LAINE SCHELIGA PRESENTS

THEY CALL ME NOONER

outskirts
press

Outskirts Press, Inc.
http://www.outskirtspress.com

ISBN: 978-1-9772-5156-5

Cover Art © 2022 by Sergey S. Voronin. All rights reserved - used with permission.

Outskirts Press and the "OP" logo are trademarks belonging to Outskirts Press, Inc.

PRINTED IN THE UNITED STATES OF AMERICA

TABLE OF CONTENTS

Chapter 1.

MEAT PIE

They call me Nooner, and there are them that'll say I ain't worth the powder to blow me to hell.

Now, for starters, this doesn't strike me as a fair estimation of a man's value. First of all, logistically, the amount of powder required to blow a man to hell is certainly questionable at best. Secondly, there's always the theological question about whether hell is where a man is headed when the blowing up is over and done with. So who's to say who's worth the powder and who ain't worth the powder? And who's to say where that feller's heading after said calculation and detonation of powder requirements? Who, indeed, save for that Hombre above? Certainly not any candy-assed Pollyanna who might choose to talk a man down behind his back.

If it was up to me to choose a proper, descriptive, all-around term for myself, I guess that phrase would be "balanced of season." By that I mean, when judging the depth and the quality of a man, one must consider the seasoning as one might in a meat pie. Properly seasoned with the correct quantity of a great variety of things, a meat pie makes for a delicious and balanced meal. Improperly balanced—for example, if you put too much spice and pepper or too much salt in the meat pie—it ain't worth a dollop of chicken shit to nobody.

I, for one, am seasoned of possum and rattlesnake meat, your desert wind and sun, your mesquite, and your dust. I'm seasoned of chewed tree bark, the marrow of unknown rodents, and river mud. I've sucked from every dried-out stream, waterin' hole, and whore's teat in this, the devil's land. I've danced your square, your rain dance, your two-step, your Cotton-Eyed Joe, and your hokey-pokey with some of the prettiest (and also some of the butt-ugliest)women you ever saw. I've pulled bullets and buckshot out of my right leg, right forearm, left butt cheek, neck, the heel of my right hand, the arch of my left foot, and my gut, mostly using an old, rusty buck knife.

Now if all of that don't serve to season a man for starters, I don't know a meat pie when I see one.

I ain't what you call popular, nor church-going, nor even particularly learned, but I have been blessed with what some womenfolk call a ruddy attractiveness, a compactness of form, and a robustness of conditioning that seems to make them likely to blush sometimes.

If the mood strikes you to put an occupation on me at the time of this writing, you might call me a scribe. But I've also worked this country as a bounty hunter, trapper, guide, prospector, horse trader, hired hand, hired gun, fence mender, water witch, rancher, dealer, gambler, bartender, and barber to name a few. All above vocations were accompanied by generally equalogical measures of success and failure, resulting in, like I say, seasoning.

The unfortunate side of all of this is that through it all, for one sorry reason or another, I've had to kill and maim more men than I have fingers and toes left to help me count. I've seen men's heads blown clean off and seen Indians and white men alike stomped one by the other into the dry desert earth by their greed and stupidity. I've been forced to hack, shoot, cut, stab, whack, poke, punch, hog-tie, and brand many who thought they might get in my way or take what I had.

I can be your best amigo or your worst nightmare come true—Satan in boots, the devil on horseback, a scarecrow of the underworld—and some will tell you I don't have a decent bone in my rotten, sore, infested, sunbaked, dust-covered body. Then again, these are probably the same sonsabitches who will tell you that I ain't worth the powder to blow me to hell. Proof positive that regardless of creed, kin, color, or clergy, some folks simply need shootin'.

Obviously this side of my seasoning don't do a bit of good for my reputation; hence, my philosophical meat-pie comparison loses some of its hearty flavor. So I don't rightly know with exactitude where the hell that leaves us.

Anyhow, by this time you're probably getting fidgety readin' all these here words. Probably asking yourself, "What the hell? Is there a goddam story in here or not?" And all I can say is just keep your shirt on and I'll get to it. In case you don't know it, there are certain formalities of which a scribing-type must dispense in order to get things properly underway.

This here story's a true one, and it's what I call an Indian-treasure-magic adventure story because there's an Indian or two in it, there's a treasure, and there's also a sort of magic in it that I can't quite explain, but maybe we can all get to understand better once I get it scratched down for us to look at and figure on.

This here story is also about making friends and losing 'em, about men caught betwixt rocks and bullets, about men gettin' greedy and dying, and there's even a bit about womenfolk that turns hard men happy whether they want to be that way or not. This last rounds out the tale in a way I couldn't have predicted, and seeing as it's every bit as true as blue, you know there ain't no way I could of made this up unless it really happened.

Chapter 2.

COFFIN VARNISH

When I rode into the Texas town called Hunkerville the first day of this saga, my legs, feet, and butt were achin' bad from being in the saddle for about a thousand years. Ain't a single thing romantic about riding a goddam horse for two weeks, no matter what those nickel cowboy books say, and my ass can tell you that.

I'd been riding idle for a time, what with having made some quick wampum on a prospecting operation some months beforehand. But now the mine had run dry, I'd been run off, and the time had come to take a hard look at my financial whereabouts and find me some work, trouble that paid, or anything in between.

By now I was right sure I'd left far enough behind this little gal named Hatty, who is without a doubt the definition of determination. Hatty's been after me for near to five years trying to loop a lariat around my dingus to keep me at a close tether. I have me a tendency to love on Hatty when I get the chance and then leave the town she's in when she starts leanin' on me with her tetherin' notions.

As I ride into Hunkerville that day, hardly nobody takes notice of me on account of it's too goddam hot for anyone to exert the energy to turn a head, except for this fat, drunk, pig-dumb head of a toad man blacksmithy working in a livery I'm passing by. I guess he's curious, and maybe looking for a customer, so he weaves out from the shade of his shack to squint me the once-over a couple of times. His face is bunched in an expression of distaste as if he'd just remembered something unpleasant he'd eaten at one time or another and didn't much relish the memory.

This fella's got hardly no hair hanging on a soot-streaked bullethead, and his teats are as big and sloppy as a fat woman, all hangin' out the front of a raggedy-ass flannel shirt full of cinder holes. As he closes in on me, I catch a serious whiff of this dainty flower. Compared to him, that livery smelled as fragrant as a rose dappled with the morning dew. I ain't exaggerating. I did a little gag and then pretended to cough on account of I didn't want to hurt this feller's feelings right up front. I wouldn't have worried about him either way except the glassiness in his eyes told me that he was probably about as drunk as a man can be without being legally dead, and I could see the mahogany handle of a big dirty Colt sticking out of his britches and hanging over his sow-colored belly, the barrel of that weapon probably nestled somewhere comfortable between his balls. I smiled as sweet as maple and gave him a careful howdy.

"We don't be likin' to havin' no strangers much aroun' here," he manages to say, unmoved by my most Christian grin.

"Well that's right cautious of you," I say, trying to get on his good side. "Town was along the way. Figured I'd stop on in, give her a look-see."

"Well, you seen all there is," he says. "So whyn't you get a move on afore somebody has to kill ya?" And with that, this big dumb toad of a man let go himself a big, weird, sissy giggle, while gently caressing the dirty grained woodhandle of that Colt.

"You run this here livery, do you?" I say, still trying my Christian best.

"Maybe do, maybe don't," says stinky toad man, snotty like.

"Well, if you do, how you gonna make any money if you threaten every bushed cowpoke comes your way that might want to make use of your outfit?"

Toad man runs a hand over the back of his neck and looks at the slime on his hand. "Hell," he says, "it's too goddam hot to work anyhow."

I looked at him for a moment or two longer, pondering his lack of industry. "So how's about you just show me where I can get some water for my horse, Shithead, and then I'll be on my way?"

His expression tightened some then. He fanned one hand over his forehead to shade his eyes from the sun, and pretended to scratch at his belly with the other. But I could see that this dirty son of a bitch was really making a slow and most deliberate move toward the handle of that big greasy Colt. "You callin' me names there, amigo?" he says.

I sighed, long and sad. "You move your goddam hand another inch toward that peashooter and you're gonna be hammering horseshoes on the cloven hooves of the devil hisself," I informed him. "Now I been riding for weeks and I'm a might tired. I could simply do with some water and maybe some goddam hospitality for me and my horse, Shithead."

Now as has been known to happen sometimes, this drunken toad of a man has made the erroneous determination that I am calling him a shithead, when in fact I am referring to the name of the less-than-noble mount that is my primary means of conveyance.

"I got yer hospipacity, you sumbitch!" shouted the toad man. He tried to draw on me, but before he could clear or I could talk some sense into him, I had my Peacemaker out clean. I put a slug just as neat as you please directly into his right eye, and it blew clean out the back of his head in a dainty mist of scarlet. He flew backward, the toad man did, and he dropped hard like an oat bag in the dust. One of his legs kicked for a moment quite unlike an oat bag, and then he died. I didn't want to shoot him; goddam I never want to shoot nobody. But as I have previously stated, some men simply need shootin'. This one in particular. And pronto.

Well, welcome all the hell to Hunkerville, Nooner, I thought to myself.

I led Shithead into the livery shack and found a trough where we both dipped our heads. Properly refreshed, I was about to lead Shithead to a stall when I heard a voice say, "You done killed Mister Looger." The voice belonged to a funny-looking kid with buggy eyes and poop on his face who was standing in the shadows by a hay chute with his finger up his nose.

"Mr. Looger was a toad man," I told that kid. "I just wanted to get some water for my horse, Shithead, and he draws on me for no dang reason. It would of been him or me."

"You ain't got to be callin' me shithead, mister," said the kid, picking away. "Mr. Looger weren't no good no how. He beat on me and Ma alla time, an' he's Ma's half brother. Smelled fierce too."

"Uh-huh," I said. "Well, quit picking your nose, kid. Ain't tidy."

But that kid kept picking away and picking away like he was digging for buried treasure or something, so I drew my Peacemaker and pushed it gently into the side of his nose. I was a bit testy by now, I got to admit.

"Goddammit boy!" I said. "Don't you understand English? Quit picking your dang nose."

The kid quit picking.

"You don't pick the banjo, do you, kid?" I holstered my gun.

"No, I ain't," kid says.

"Well, you got a good start if ever you decide to," I told him. "Now how's about putting up my horse, Shithead, give him a good brushing, and tie a feedbag on him," I said. I tossed the kid a coin.

"Oke," says the kid, shaking his head and leading Shithead away. "Except you ain't need be callin' me shithead alla time."

I sighed at what was becoming a near regular misunderstanding of communication. I slapped some of the trail dust off myself and set about to dragging Mr. Looger to a place where he wouldn't be quite so noticeable. Then I made my way across the road from the livery to what looked to be a saloon. There was a sign over the door that said "Bill's De-luxe Saloon" on it, but mostly it was just a dirt-box shed with flies buzzing around the cool of the entrance and not too much "de-luxe" about it that I could immediately determine. There was a blanket for a door, and as I reached up to push it aside, some poor old son of a bitch comes flying out of the place and T-bones me with his head where I'm standing and knocks me backassward into the street. As I fall, I grab the guy by the shoulders, and he's looking down at me with eyes as red as blood and clutching at me and making faces and screaming, "Get 'em offa me! Get 'em off! There's June bugs on me! Eeeeeeee! June bugs! June bugs! Get them goddam things off of me; they're big as bullets!"

"Easy! Take her easy there," I said, confused and not knowing what to do 'cause there was no indication whatever of a June bug or any other some such bug anywhere in the immediate area.

But this fella wriggled and squiggled in my grasp anyhow, grabbling in an attempt to reach all parts of his body at the same time. "You don't see them goddam bugs?" He screeched. "Big as bullets, they are. Get 'em off me! Scorpions too! Big, mean sonsabitches. *Get 'em offa me!*"

He started slapping at himself some more, and still wiggling and squiggling around, he fell to his knees, clutching my leg. "Oh my Lord," he said, squeezing, "please, please, mister. Get 'em offa me. I'm beggin' ya."

Well I've seen this type of behavior before. This fella had what I figured to be a terribly serious case of the whiskey jim-jams. So I did the logical thing. I took off his hat and started whacking him with it.

"Here you go," I said. "Here you go now. I got 'em. I got 'em." I whacked him good on his back and his chest and his face until his hat was as shapeless as a whore's panty. "There you go," I said. "There you go. I got them goddam critters. Every one."

"Get that one." He pointed to himself. "Get it! Get that one!"

And so I slapped him a little more with his hat where he pointed until he seemed satisfied. Then the man stood and, quite composed now, took back his cover, put a fist into it to give it some fresh shape, and crammed it back on his head.

"Much obliged," he said, stamping his feet. "My name's Bill Teetle, and I am the proprietor of this fine establishment, Bill's De-luxe Saloon."

"They call me Nooner," I said, "Dade Nooner."

And we shook hands.

"Deeply grateful for your assistance," said Bill Teetle, "and I do not mean to be abrupt, but I'm afraid I must go promptly with no time to chat in this interim. I have an appointment to see my physician, you see, for I have something unusual growing on my balls."

I nodded in complete understanding.

And turning on his boot heel, Bill Teetle reeled away down the street.

As I said, the saloon was a sorry affair to behold, and even sorrier on the inside—nothing more than a shack with a dirt floor, a coupla splintery tables and chairs tossed around, and a picture of a naked lady in garters on the wall with about a thousand bullet holes in it. A scowling, wrinkly prick that I took to be the bartender hunkered over a plank of wood that was settled on two barrels. I guess this was supposed to be the de-luxe part of the bar area. He looked me over like I was a vagrant or something equally below his station. Sure, I was a dusty sight to see having been on the trail so long and all, but that barkeep didn't look all that great either what with a greasy, lopsided moustache; an old, ripped burlap shirt; and fingernails as dirty as if he'd been digging around in a buffalo's bunghole. Still, I figured that we'd get along just fine soon's I showed him I had me some wampum for whiskey and the potential to provide a generous gratuity besides, provided the service was adequate.

I looked slowly over my right shoulder and saw three men sitting behind me, watching me close as I jingled in. They were sitting on dynamite boxes in the corner at a pitiful excuse for a table and playing at poker, piling up matches instead of chips, and smoking some kinda stinky tobaccy. I watched them for a while, smiling and nodding, and then I leaned toward the barkeep on the old piece of dry-rotted plank and slapped some silver down.

"How do?" I say.

"What you want?" snaps the barkeep, looking down snooty on my coin.

"Well, looky what the pig dragged in," says one of them cowboys behind my back. Everybody in the place, that being the three cowboys and the barkeep, had themselves a laugh like this was the funniest thing they ever heard on earth in the entirety of their goddam lives.

I turned toward the cowboy who was laughing the loudest and gave him the hard eye. He was a big old boy with a long black beard and a face that was as soot-covered as a campfire log.

"I don't want no trouble from no trail shitcakes," I said with my most Christian grin. "You boys just keep on playing your game and keep your noses out of my ass and we'll get along just fine." Don't know why I said that part about my ass, but it seemed confusing and nasty enough to pipe 'em down.

Then I turned back to the barkeep. "I just want me some whiskey," I told him. "And it'd be nice if you'd show me some conviviality with your service."

"What kind of whiskey you want?" the barkeep barked, now with considerable impatience.

"What kind you got?"

The barkeep sighed as if I were asking him to reveal the secret of ancient Arab arithmetic or some other such complexity.

"We got Tiger Spit," he said, "and Tangle Leg, Scorpion Tongue Oil, Coffin Varnish, and Popskull. Popskull's extra," he added.

"How you make your Popskull?" I inquired.

"The reg'lar way, goddammit," he snaps.

"And what is that then? The reg'lar way?"

"Tobacco, molasses, red chili peppers, raw alcyhol, burned sugar, and gunpowder. If you *really* need to know," he says, still snooty.

"What's in your Tangle Leg?" I prodded further.

The barkeep made a face and produced a profound exasperated farting sound with his lips. "Tobacco, molasses, red chili peppers, raw alcyhol, and burned sugar," he replied, when his farting sound was through.

"So basically," I said, "you're withholding the gunpowder in the Tangle Leg."

"Basically," said the barkeep.

I was considering the epicurean aspects of gunpowder versus no gunpowder in my whiskey when I hear a snort behind me. Then I heard another of them cowboys say in a stuttery voice, "S-s-s-say, l-looky here n-n-now. L-l-l-looky here. L-l-l-ooks like we got us a *fancy* d-d-d-d-drinkin' gentleman here in our very midst."

"And it looks," I said, turning to look over my shoulder,

"like dog turds can learn the English language."

I turned back to the barkeep. "What does old Mr. Bill Teetle like to drink when he comes to grace the confines of his enterprise?" I asked.

"Coffin Varnish," said the barkeep. "Mr. Teetle favors the Varnish. You know William Teetle, do you?"

"One of my best amigos of all time," I said. "Give me a shot of whatever Mr. William Teetle enjoys."

The barkeep smiled at me for the first time.

"Well, any friend of William Teetle's is a friend of mine," he said, suddenly gracious as hell. He poured me a good-sized snootful of cloudy brown Coffin Varnish in an old dirty jar and slid it my way. It often pays to make personal references to people in high places, whether they got imaginary June bugs or not.

I packed away the Coffin Varnish in a big gulp. Right away, my eyes started watering, my chest started heaving, and the tips of my fingers went numb. I did a little dance, hacking and coughing and jingling around in a circle, whacking my chest with my fists. Once I started breathing normally, I smiled.

"She's a smoothie," I tell the barkeep.

"Ain't she?" he says.

I notice his eyes are wandering behind me and the trigger finger on his right hand is twitching for no good reason. Then I feel someone breathing down my neck, and a doofy voice behind me says, "What'd you call my friend, stranger?"

I turn slow, and that big bearded cowboy that I was talking about before is standing in my face now, breathing his stinky breath on me. His arms are at his sides and bent a little at the elbows in an offensive posture; his sky blue eyes are staring at me hard, and his thick, raggedy-ass, critter-infested black beard is hanging in my face.

"I called him a dog turd," I say. "And do me a favor and quit breathing on me, wouldja? Jesus howdy, big man, you could knock a dead hog off a shitpile with that stinky breath you got there."

"Name's Pine Top McGee," says the big man, trying to hold tough, "on account of I'm big. I got me a bad tooth. That over there is Cheese Dinkle, and that there is Nub Henderson. Neither one of us ain't no dog turd. I don't think you ought to be talkin' on us like that."

Out the corner of my eye I could see them other two cowboys sniggering and giggling like a couple of schoolgirls, and I figured that they put this big simpleton up to what could have amounted to an unfortunate conclusion.

"Seems you shitcakes got to talking in a rather obtuse manner firsthand," I observed carefully to the Pine Top.

This observation didn't seem to register too well with Pine Top right away. He growled and tried to draw on me, but he was so slow it wasn't even a contest. I didn't even have the heart to shoot him, he was so slow and drunk and dumb. Instead, before he could clear his holster with his Wesson, my sawed-off was out from under my poncho and pressed firm into his throat. He made a little squeaking noise that sounded something like "weeeeeg," and he put his hands in the air.

"Okay now, easy does it there, Pine Top McGee," I said. "Drop that hot handle o' yours real slow. And tell them giggly boys over there to do the same and kick their guns my way."

"Ow," he squeaked, his big hairy chin high in the air. "I wan't gonna shoot ya for real. Ow! Ooo! I was only supposed to put some scare in ya is all."

"Well, you scared me all right," I said. "My body is wracked with terror. Now do as I say, unless you want to see your vocal chords hanging on the walls like Christmas jerky."

Pine Top nodded at them other cowboys and a couple of guns came tumbling nearby over the dirt floor. I pointed my sawed-off at Pine Top's nuggets while I leaned over to pick them up. I put them on the bar.

"Don't get no ideas now, barkeep," I warned him. He had his hands high too and was shaking like a squirrel passing peach pits.

"No ideas here," he confirmed.

"Okay," I said. "Now, suppose you and me and the boys play us a little card game." I pushed Pine Top in the direction of the table with my sawed-off. "High card wins," I told him.

"Huh?"

"Cut the deck. You take the high card on the cut and I won't have to shoot your big dumb ass."

I'm not sure that Pine Top fully understood the intricacies of this card game proposal, but he gave me a bewildered smile, leaned over the poker table, and cut the pile, holding up a king.

"Look," he said, pretty certain that things were going his way.

"Nice," I said. Then I nodded at one of the other cowboys, the one called Nub. He was a rangy dude with a big nose that had something wrong with it because it was all lumpy and purple and a chunk of it was missing. Trembling with rage, Nub cut the deck to a queen.

"He lost," I said to Pine Top. "Shoot him."

"Huh?" said Pine Top, totally confused now.

"The hell you say," Nub responded angrily.

"He drew less than you," I explained to Pine Top. "You got to shoot him."

Pine Top shook his head and nodded at Nub. "I don't like Nub much," he said. "But I don't want to shoot him much either."

"Those are the rules," I said. "You gonna play by the rules or what?" I spun the cylinder of my gun, removing all the bullets save one, and handed him my Colt.

Pine Top was obviously as bewildered as a simpleton can be. He thought about it a minute or so more, looking from me to Nub and back to me again. Then he shrugged, aimed, closed his eyes, and managed to shoot Nub in the foot. This sent Nub Henderson skittering and screeching away and out of the saloon.

The room was full of smoke and the sharp smell of spent powder. "Now *you* draw a card," I said to the fellow who remained at the table.

The remaining puncher, the one they called Cheese, was meaner looking still. He had a cloudy, dead-looking right eye and pock marks that made his face look like the sponge I use to clean myself off with at Miss Aggie's Whore and Steak House in Houston. "Draw one now," I said.

"I ain't g-g-g-g-gonna draw one," says Cheese, crossing his arms.

"I'll shoot you if you don't," I said, pressing my sawed-off into his chest. "Those are the rules."

"I d-d-d-don't know if I feel quite right about these here r-r-r-rules in the first place," says the pocked-up cowboy Cheese, whose head jerks around and who tends to spit some when he talks.

Pine Top was still trying to figure the angles of this new game too, counting on his fingers and looking perplexedly at the ceiling.

I waited.

"Hey, wait a minute! How come you don't cut the c-c-c-cards?" Cheese wanted to know. "It's your turn to c-c-cut the goddam c-c-cards!"

"Yeah. How come you ain't cuttin' 'em?" says Pine Top.

"Well, all right," I said, and I did. I cut the cards. But I didn't let them punchers have a look at the card I cut to right away. I studied the card a minute with a thoughtful look on my face and then casually put it in my shirt breast pocket.

"I'll make you a deal," I said. "You boys want to call it quits right now, you give me a hundred dollars and I won't have to shoot you."

Cheese made a long, expectorating sound, very similar to the one the barkeep had produced earlier in my narration. "We ain't g-g-g-got no hunnerd dollars," Cheese said. "Show us yer g-g-g-goddam card."

"All we gots is matches," said Pine Top forlornly.

"So what do you expect me to do on this?" I said. "Rules are rules, after all."

"Well," babbled Pine Top, who by now was entirely beside himself with vexation, "I can show you where you can find hunnerds and hunnerds o' dollars in Injun gold. How'd that be?"

"Awww," said dead-eye Cheese. "Pine Top, you big d-d-d-dumbass! W-what you g-g-go and tell this here s-s-s-stranger about the g-g-g-gold for? He ain't even showed us his card!"

"Well then, I will." I said. I pulled the planted ace I always carry in my shirt breast pocket and tossed it face up on the table. "Suppose we all hold off on the shooting and settle into some civil conversation."

I had actually drawn the deuce of clubs. But it remained undisturbed in my shirt pocket.

Chapter 3.

TIPTOE SAM

Later, after a series of whiskeys and the sulky objections of Cheese, I managed to prod and decipher Pine Top's vernacular concerning a Comanche Indian treasure that he'd heard about from some hunchbacked Apache he knew named Tiptoe Sam. Pine Top told the following story, which I must admit I have taken certain liberties to tidy and embellish in order to encourage brevity:

Through years of travel and plunder over the Great Plains, Comanche warriors came to accumulate bits of rare natural minerals they discovered upon the land: gold, turquoise, topaz, malachite, and silver, among many other colorful stones of greater or lesser value. They would gather these treasures, which they called the "stones of color," and at each moon would present their finds in the audience of the great chiefs. The ceremony was supposed to be a symbol of the kindness of the earth and the generosity of the gods. The idea was that the more stones of color the Comanche could accumulate, the more favorable the Comanche gods would be.

Some of the stones of color were made into ornaments and decorated the most powerful in the tribe, while the rest were hidden away by tribe elders in a cave or a hollow or some such sacred place. Somewhere along the line, the stones of color were lost or stolen, and no one ever found out what happened to them. After that, a great period of decline beset the Comanche nation. According to Pine Top though, this crazy hunchbacked Apache Tiptoe Sam said he knew where the stones of color could be found, on account of Tiptoe Sam was the one who stole them in the first place. And now, for some reason, Tiptoe Sam was of a mind to return to the place where he hid these treasures all those years ago and reclaim them.

Of course, the story sounds dubious to me. Men with a skin full tend to spout finely embellished tales of wealth and adventure when somebody else is paying for the Popskull. But I get to thinking, what the hell? I ain't got nothin' else to do for the time being. And besides, in spite of myself, I'm starting to take a little shine to these ugly hombres, especially Pine Top. Nothing unusual like being in jail for a long time or anything, mind you, but I was just gettin' that feeling that you get when you think maybe you might have met somebody that you can talk to, have a few laughs with, and won't have to kill right away.

And so that was how the three of us—that being me, Cheese Dinkle, and Pine Top McGee—decided to mount up and ride to the place where that hunchbacked Apache named Tiptoe Sam made his home to see if there was any credibility to this claim. I was hoping maybe Sam wouldn't mind if we tagged along in his search for the stones of color.

Pine Top informed me that Tiptoe Sam might be kind of tough to get anything out of at first on account of he's got a roundabout way of saying things and he gets even more long-winded when he can get at some whiskey. But fate will deal her cards as she will, and you got to play them cards as they lay. Those are the rules.

So we rode, and as we did, Pine Top was trying to convince Cheese of my notoriety. Cheese still hadn't taken much of a liking to me, and I figured he probably wouldn't for a time because he wasn't what you'd call an outgoing, sociable type in the first place.

"Come on, Cheese," said Pine Top. "This here is Dade Nooner. Dade Nooner! He's nearly famous and all. He been done writ up in them nickel cowboy books!"

I am pleased that Pine Top had heard of me. Of course, if you haven't heard of me, you've probably been tuggin' your dingus in a lean-to somewhere for most of your adult life.

As men tend to do when they're going someplace, we ride. We're about five miles out of Hunkerville when we come upon an old, beat-up teepee set up before a bitty fire right smack dab in the middle of no place. We get off our horses. Actually, me and Pine Top are the only ones riding horses. Cheese is riding an old mule that he alternately names Son of a Bitch, Stubborn Bastard, and Goddam Idjit.

Pine Top approaches the raggedy teepee carefully and hollers some. "Hey, Sam," he yells. "Tiptoe Sam! It's me! It's Pine Top! Don't shoot now!" Then Pine Top says to me kind of quiet like, "Don't make no sudden moves, Nooner. Sam's some jumpy."

I watch the teepee for a while, and after a minute or so, I spot an old, wrinkly red man poke his head slowly from around the back of it. He's hunched over, as are most hunchbacks, and he's wearing this magnificent buffalo coat lined with sheepskin even though it's about a thousand degrees out. I notice that the coat is so long that it drags around in the dirt. A rifle suddenly appears, and I find myself looking down the bore of a buffalo gun that's as big around as a hitching post.

"What do you want?" demands Tiptoe Sam.

"It's us, Sam," says Pine Top again, raising his hands. "Pine Top and Cheese Dinkle from Hunkerville. We brought us a friend."

Sam doesn't say anything but instead points his big gun in the air and lets off a helluva round. It explodes with a most powerful report that I can feel in my chest. Then Sam starts running around the teepee doing some kind of a dance and laughing crazy and making a wailing sound. He is hunched over and I figure he must be about four feet tall. I figure right there and then that old hunchbacked Tiptoe Sam is probably about as undone as a lizard at a clog dance. But then again, first impressions are often unreliable.

Eventually Sam gets tired of running around the teepee and he drops his gun and squats down slow in front of the fire. I notice that Sam is bare-ass naked underneath that skin coat of his, and his big ol' dingus is hanging out loose and long like a sleeping one-eyed snake in the dust.

"Okay," says Cheese. "W-w-w-w-we're comin' over now, Sam, so you jes' take her easy now. Easy as she g-g-g-goes then, old b-b-b-buddy."

Pine Top nods the go-ahead to me, and together we all start making our way over to Tiptoe Sam nice and slow. Then we squat across from him at the fire.

"Ah, Pine Top man. Good to see." Sam nods to the big man with a warm familiarity. He glances at Cheese and he makes that all purpose and familiar farting sound with his lips. Then Sam looks at me hard and long with sharp green eyes that seem to burn directly into my skull. His gaze makes me feel a might uneasy, I got to admit, although I try not to show my discomfort by looking square back at him and putting my most Christian grin to work. He has long black braids, Sam has, that hang over a face that's dark brown and shiny like a walnut, and he wears a remarkable necklace around his throat on a tough cord of rawhide. On this cord is strung a slew of what look to be glass beads and feathers, and in the middle of the whole doodad hangs a solid gold nugget the size of a baby's fist. It must've weighed ten ounces easy.

"My golly, look at that nugget you got there, Sam," I say.

"Every time I see it, I get excited," whispers Pine Top.

Meanwhile Sam is still looking me over.

"What is your name?" he asks me.

"They call me Nooner," I respond.

"Hmmm." Sam nods. "Yes, Nooner. I know of you."

"I been around," I say by way of explanation.

"Nooner has been many places," Sam tells me. "He has been the friend of the Indian, where other men have turned away."

"Well, don't go overboard with it, Sam," I say. "I shot me a few Injuns too."

Sam smiles, showing me three teeth, white as ivory. "A few need shooting," he says.

I nod and he nods as we come to this deep and mutual understanding. Then he stands, pats me on the back, mumbles something I can't figure, and gets to running around the teepee again, making that keening noise some more.

"What the hell is he doing?" I ask Cheese with incredulity.

"I d-d-d-dunno what n-n-n-no Injun's doin'," says Cheese in exasperation.

By this time I am starting to get a little impatient. Indian tradition or no, this whole dancing and hollering ceremonial business wears thin.

"Godammit! Knock it the hell off, Sam," I yell at him. "We want to talk to you and get somethin' done. We sure the hell can't do it while you're dancing."

Surprisingly, Sam knocks it off. He stands upright, and his eyebrows knit together. "Okay," he says. Then he wanders back over to us and squats down at the fire again.

At that we settled into conversation.

"These here boys tell me that you might be able to use a party to recover some Comanche rocks or something of that nature," I said.

"Humma," says Sam, raising an eyebrow as he gazed into the fire.

"And these boys have invited me to be the trail boss in the search for this treasure, provided you're so inclined."

"We d-d-d-din't make you no b-b-boss," objected Cheese.

"Sure you did," I said, showing Cheese the business end of

my sawed-off.

"Okay, b-b-b-boss," said Cheese.

"So where can we find this here treasure?" I asked Sam, cutting to the chase.

Sam smirked. Then he closed his eyes and raised his hands palm up to the sky.

"Treasure is easy to find but never easy to know," Sam said. "Most men cannot find it, for they do not know it even when it is in front of their noses. Even when it is theirs to take."

"Well, hell, that m-m-makes a lot of sense," said Cheese irritably.

Sam continued, "Treasure for Nooner is where the wind speaks free and calm through the tall trees. Umma-umma-umma. Treasure is in a place where the water runs clear and cold and good. Treasure is in a place where the heart is suddenly glad. Treasure is where the lone wolf howls for joy in the night, for the wolf has finally returned to home and companion. The wolf cries in gladness."

"Ah," I said in deep consideration of this. "And where exactly would that place be, Sam?"

Sam looked a little annoyed. "It is in a green place where the riding comes to an end. It is where the snow never comes. It is where the land is peaceful and the wind speaks soft and free through the high trees."

"You covered that wind-speaking trees part already," I said.

Sam shrugged. "I like that part," he said.

Sam scratched himself and adjusted his dingus. Then he lifted his palms skyward again. "In the time of Cochise, as a young brave, Sam meets a beautiful Comanche squaw," he said. "Her name is Wickey-Wickey. She smiles upon Sam. Sam captures a mighty cat and gives the skin to her. He follows Wickey-Wickey to a secret place where the Comanche stones of color are hidden. Wickey-Wickey does not see Sam follow. She steals a stone from ancient treasure for necklace for Sam to wear. This stone." And he held out the gold nugget that hung about his neck. "Then we did something," Sam continued. "But Comanche tribe is ashamed for Wickey-Wickey, for Sam has a body that is crooked."

"What the h-h-hell is that c-c-c-crazy Injun saying?" said Cheese. I gave Cheese the stink eye and motioned for him to shut his piehole. "Shut yer piehole," I told him.

"The Comanche fear Tiptoe Sam for he has much magic," said Sam. "Tribe makes Wickey-Wickey spurn Sam's love." At this the old man's eyes became rheumy and filled with tears.

"Busted your heart, did she, Sam?" I said gently.

"In many small pieces," Sam concurred.

"And you know where the treasure is hidden?"

"Yes. Because after the heartbreaking, Sam steals away the Comanche stones of color and hides them in a place only Sam knows. It was not a good thing to do."

"Is this place far away?" I ask.

"Near and far."

"What direction?"

"North," Sam says and smiles. "To the soft wind, Nooner Boss. Where the snow never comes. Where the grasses are green. That is where the treasure can be found for Nooner."

"Where the water runs clear and fresh and cold. And where the wolf cries in the night joyfully upon his return to home and companion," I added.

"And where the heart is suddenly glad," said Sam. "Nooner learns well."

"Umma-umma-umma," I said.

Sam laughed. "Sam will show Cheese man with the smell and the large Pine Tree man and the Nooner Boss treasure," he said. "Sam gets old and has things he must do. Sam must do a thing before he dies. But he cannot do it alone."

"Are we about d-d-d-done here?" said Cheese, always annoyed, annoying and impatient.

"Sam will show the way, but we must do the right thing.

Men must do a thing for Sam."

"Name it," I said.

"Nooner must help Sam find Wickey-Wickey. And other things."

"Fair enough," I said.

Sam nodded his head and smiled again, fingering that chunk of gold nugget hanging heavy around his neck as though he were drawing something from it.

Chapter 4.

TWILIGHT

I talked to Sam for quite a while after that, but he was by no means specific, not being what you might call any road map to riches by a long shot. He was being cagey, which I guess is smart. You tell someone too much about where a lot of treasure can be found these days, and sure as hell you'll find yourself real still lying and drying in the sun while someone else is wearing out your boots and spending your loot.

Most of what Sam says by now is babble, but you can't knock it. I learned a long time ago that babble often has a basis in fact once you untangle what it all means.

I send Pine Top and Cheese back into Hunkerville to pick up some supplies for a journey I wildly estimate will take us a month or so. After they've gone, I sidle up to Sam for a little more conversation. Night is falling by now, the cool of the twilight punctuated by the squeaks and beeps and howls of night critters. Bats have started to flit overhead in the nightfall, drawn by bugs attracted to the popping fire.

"You got whiskey?" Sam asked after Cheese and Pine Top had ridden off.

"Sure," I told him. I had had my flask filled by that snooty bartender in Hunkerville. I pulled a flagon from my saddlebag, squatted at the fire, and held the flask out to him.

We both shared tugs from the jug and were silent for a while, feeding sticks to the flames, letting the whiskey warm us, and watching the night as it fell to the ground. Eventually we got to talking again in our way about this and that and the other thing, each of us making an effort to understand the other. It wasn't easy at first, but after a time I found, curiously enough, that the less we spoke, the more we seemed to say. I wish this characteristic of conversation applied to more of us.

One thing about Sam is that when he gets liquored up some or bored and tired of talking, he starts diggin' in the dirt or dancing or making things out of sticks. It's okay with me, seeing as if I was alone in the plains with nothing to do, I'd probably make things out of sticks and dig in the dirt too.

Eventually, Cheese and Pine Top get back with a load of supplies for our trip: jerky, hardtack, flour, coffee, and so forth. We put up the horses and the mule for the night, cook up a little coffee, and, figuring we can't do much more until morning, turn in. Sam disappears inside his teepee.

Just before I dropped off that first night, in my head I was seeing a bag of my very own gold nuggets as big as peyote buttons and imagining all the wonderful things I was going to buy with them. Then, just minutes before I dropped off comfortable, I got to thinking about that miracle of a woman, Hatty, and wondering where she was and what she was up to and what dumb trail boy was grabbing at her and what she might say if I showed up one day on her doorstep with a big bag of gold. But I only thought about this for a minute or two because by then I was sound asleep.

Chapter 5.

RATTLESNAKES AND HORNY TOADS

I didn't even hear the rattler or feel it climbing on me as I woke up that next morning. But I did hear a blood-curdling whoop when all of a sudden, as my eyes popped open, I saw Sam's grinning face over me, and he was holding on to the business end of the fattest old rattler I ever saw in my life. I've got to admit I almost went winky right then and there in my bedroll.

Sam holds the rattler up to the sky—that big, fat, mean snake—and it's coiling madly around his arm and rattling away and showing its fangs, and it's as big around as an ear of corn and as long as a bootlace.

"Jesus howdy!" I think I exclaimed as I jumped from the bedroll.

Sam was delighted, stroking and petting and in general playing around with the deadly snake like it was nothing more than a lively coil of rope.

"Nooner is lucky," said Tiptoe Sam. "Snakes are good. Much magic. Nooner brings luck to Sam and Wickey-Wickey." And with that, Sam trotted off with that snake and disappeared into his teepee with it.

Everybody's pretty much up by now, Pine Top and Cheese scared to terrified wide-awakeness by Sam's whooping. I am still shaken some, but eventually we all regain our composure and get to alternately scratchin' our heads and other places and breaking wind and making other good-morning noises that men tend to make.

"D-d-d-don't like that c-c-c-crazy Injun," whines Cheese as he squirts in a bush.

"What do you suppose he's gonna do with that snake?" I ponder aloud.

"I d-d-dunno what no Injun does with no snake," says Cheese in his predictable, exasperated rancor.

Cheese and Pine Top get to mixing up some flour and water for biscuits, and we have some coffee. Eventually we eat and strike the camp. Sam emerges from his teepee and helps himself to a biscuit. Then he drops his teepee and loads everything he owns into a bunch of hemp bags and hefts the mess of them onto a stick travois that he ties to his back. No sign of the snake. I figure maybe Sam had it for breakfast.

Sam comes up to me and pats me on the shoulder and shows me his three teeth. He's still wearing that big buffalo coat and he's sweating, but I notice he has an odor about him that is much like the smell of fresh-cut cedar. I don't know how he managed it, but Sam was always about the least rank of all of us through the whole trip that was to follow. Pine Top smelled pretty strong being the burly man he is and having a bad tooth and all, and I couldn't stand to be around Cheese for much more than an hour without starting to gag. Aside from his complexion, I was beginning to comprehend from whence Cheese derived his odiferous name.

We head out on our journey full of hope and expectation, Cheese riding on Goddam Idjit, the mule; me on Shithead, the brown-headed roan; Pine Top on Dangle-Not, the gelding; and Sam on foot leading the way at a remarkable trot and dragging his worldly possessions stick-wise behind him.

We haven't gone but about a mile or so when we come upon another rattler lying on a rock in the sun, and quick as a cat with that war whoop of his, Sam captures this snake too. He holds it up to the sky and goes through similar ministrations as before; mumbles some; and then drops the thing, fangs and all, into his hemp bag. Then he tosses the bag onto the travois with the rest of his crap and cuts out again in his fast canter.

For a few days, the trip was unincident prone. We'd cover about ten miles or so in a day, break, make camp, eat biscuits and jerky, drink coffee, tell tall tales, sleep, wake up, eat, poop, and then continue the next day the same as before with Sam as our guide.

The land was taking on a little more life as we moved northward. The flat and desolate sands of the desert gave way to sweet grasses, sage, creosote, and Joshua. On the fifth day, the weather broke, and we found ourselves in a rain shower that soaked us to the skin and loosened our dispositions considerable. As the dust of the land turned to mud, we stripped down buck naked and did ourselves our own little rain dance after the fact, letting the fresh drops rinse some of the big chunks off of our bodies in refreshing fashion. Then the rain was gone as fast as she came.

By now, Cheese is complaining a good deal more of the time, even though we haven't been out but for much than a week. I am to learn that Cheese isn't ideal to have around in the way of travel, what with his whining, scrimping on the work, and trying to cut corners whenever he can and eating more than his share. Pine Top is a hearty traveling companion though, handy with a hand and the last to turn in. Sam keeps to himself pretty much, except when he decides to dig in the dirt, steal a nip of my whiskey, study the sky for direction, grab a rattler, or make things out of sticks.

To help pass the time, I take the occasional opportunity to show off a little on the trail. I've been blessed with a special sharpness of eyesight, compliments of my great-grandfather Spooner Nooner. It's got me out of more trouble than the twin Peacemakers my daddy give me.

"You want to see some shooting, boys?" I asked one day as we rode.

"Sure," says Pine Top.

I reined up on Shithead and dismounted.

"You see that horny toad up ahead about a hundred yards or so on that rock outcrop under that cactus?" I asked.

Pine Top squints. "Nope," he says.

"Yes, I see toad," said Sam, hand over brow.

"I d-d-d-don't see a god-d-d-dang thing," whined Cheese.

I drew a careful Peacemaker bead and let loose a shot. "Aha," I said.

"Aha what?" said Cheese.

"Follow me," I said, mounting up.

Pretty soon we were at the spot where that horny toad was sunning himself. He was still on that rock, most of that toad anyhow, except now one of his horns was missing.

"Hoo-ey! That's some dern shooting," said Pine Top with proper admiration.

Even Sam was duly impressed. Cheese scowled, and on we rode.

Chapter 6.

ELISHUA B. TOMBATU
THE THIRD

About ten days into the journey, Cheese is really starting to get on my nerves, and I'm nearly of a mind to shoot him in the jaw just to shut him up. I know for a fact that he's been swiping an occasional jerky or two more than his share, and he complains on the trail all the time like a whore with a hole in her stocking. Tiptoe Sam ain't complaining, and he's on foot. Pine Top ain't complaining, and I sure the hell ain't complaining either.

"Awww," complains Cheese. "How c-c-c-come it's always so goddam hot? I'm all itchin' and all. I'm s-s-startin' not to care about n-no treasure. My b-butt hurts me bad!"

"How come you just don't shut up, Cheese?" says Pine Top, who is getting fretful just hearing about anything Cheese has to say anymore. "How come?"

"Shut your whiny piehole," I mumble.

"Cheese man should keep tongue in head," adds Sam.

Now Cheese is of a mind to take criticism from me and even from Pine Top until the pigs come home to roost, but the fact that what he considers a lowly Injun might make such a remark puts the pock-marked son of a bitch over the top.

Cheese is suddenly as enraged as he can be, and he gets to sputtering and spitting like he always does when he gets mad and tries to talk. "D-d-d-don't you be t-t-talkin' like that to m-m-me, you dirty dog Injun!" Cheese bellows. He yanks a pistola out of his holster and draws a bead. "I'll shoot you where you s-s-s-stand and see you in hell, you red-skin s-s-s-son of a bitch!"

Now none of this even caused a ruffle in the demeanor of Tiptoe Sam, who stood in his usual hunkered way smiling down the barrel of Cheese's sidearm, unafraid and, in fact, entirely entertained.

"Ha," laughed Sam. "You make many laughs for me, Cheese man of the stink. Ho!"

Both of my Peacemakers were well in hand before I even had much time to think about it, both of them pointing with purpose at Cheese's cloudy eye. I'd had enough of this stinking trail cake, and my bottled frustration had reached the cork-poppin' point.

"Give me an excuse to drop you, Cheese," I said quietly. "Hurt one hair on Sam's red head and you're as dead as a bacon pig."

Meanwhile, Sam was still laughing like a lunatic. "Ha, ho. Ha!"

Cheese took a hard look at the two guns drawn down on him and, whimpering, holstered his gun. "I d-d-didn't mean nothin' by it, Nooner," Cheese mumbled by way of apology.

Pine Top looked at me and shook his head.

And on we rode.

As we moved through ever-changing rocky territory, suddenly and, as always, for no apparent reason, Sam let out another cry, bent to the earth, dropped to his knees, and began running his hands through the dirt. He picked something up; an enormous, steaming range muffin it was. Running it through his fingers, he broke it up, squeezed it, held it to the sky, sniffed it, then let it fall.

"New," he said brightly.

"Looks used to me," said Pine Top.

"I could have told you it was fresh, Sam," I said. "I wouldn't of had to pick the thing up and squeeze it and all such."

"One horse nearby," said Sam, brushing his hands on his buffalo coat. "A large horse, a tall man. And a wagon."

"We'd better keep a sharp eye then. And ride softly, hombres," I said.

And we did, our eyes peeled some sharper as we went along. We came to a rise and worked up to where we could see a small tree-studded plain that stretched for ten miles or more in a northerly direction. In a clearing by a red rock outcrop, we could make out the figure of a horse sipping from a little creek, and a ways from the horse teetered a crazy, crooked, circus-like painted wagon. The wagon was an impressive sight to see, rendered pink and yellow with all manner of character, design, and doodad painted upon it, with dangling pots and pans and other such housewares clanking in the breeze. It was a most frivolous combination of color and collection that was as entertaining to the eye as it was challenging to a man's sense of order. Two of its big wooden wheels were settled beneath the wagon, suggesting a broken axle.

"Medicine wagon?" wondered Cheese.

"Looks to be something like that," I said. "Better we investigate careful. Sam, you and Pine Top circle and move on it from behind. Me and Cheese'll take either flank. Any trouble, shoot twice in the air."

"Okay," said Sam. Then he was gone running in a cloud of dust before I could say Flapjack Bertha, with Pine Top not far behind.

I move in on the wagon, circling round behind the cluster

of red rock for cover. When I start to get close, I hear a sweet sound on the wind that can't be anything but echophone music. It's a tender rendition of the much beloved temperance song "Lord Keep Me on That Wagon."

Then I see a man. He's tall, lanky, and black as coal, with white whiskers and that sort of sucked-in countenance that undertakers seem to have. His limbs look too long for his torso but seem to work with clever economy anyhow, keeping him balanced high on a rock with his legs crossed. A dented top hat sets square in the middle of his head. He has on blue and white striped pantaloons and red braces with no shirt, and he's playing that echophone as if his poor heart was about to bust from melancholy.

I jump off Shithead, slap his butt, and send the horse across the camp for distraction. The man watches Shithead run by, but he doesn't lose a beat in his tune or get up or jump or even say boo. Rather, he just keeps playing on that mouth organ. I approach the man from the side, and when I get to within whistling distance, I yell at him.

"You play with skill, stranger," I said.

The man nodded, but kept on playing.

"I say, you play that thing with skill. Suppose you know that song 'Sweet Beckoning Sue'? Do you?"

The man lifted his head to nod again, but he kept right on playing.

"I've of a mind to hear 'Sweet Beckoning Sue'," I said again, with a bit more emphasis.

By this time I had moved nearly within spitting distance. But the man continued to ignore me. Only after he had finished his song to a long and satisfying conclusion did he lower his echophone. He began tapping the instrument against the palm of his hand to knock the spit loose, and then he lifted his head to eyeball me straight for the first time. His eyes had the unexpected color of a nickel derringer.

"I was told by my father years ago," said the man in a

funny foreign accent, "that a man is at his best when he sees things through to a proper conclusion."

"No interruption intended," I said.

"When you're playing for the mighty Amun-Ra, it is best to give your best and most complete performance," he said.

"Understood," I replied, not understanding.

The man smiled, then lowered his head and started playing a rendition of "Sweet Beckoning Sue." And I swear it was a reading the likes of which I haven't heard before or since. It was a performance sprinkled somehow with the flavor of gospel notes and some heart-tugging notes and some clogging notes thrown in here and there too. Pretty soon all of us were gathered around this curious fellow in a kind of unexplainable musical ecstasy. We all got to dancing and stomping and raisin' up dust together in a pure and nearly magical joy that the stranger's music conjured up within us.

And when that fellow was done playing, Pine Top and Cheese and me start applauding to show our appreciation. Sam continued to dance because he just liked to dance around anyhow, music or not, while the curious man meantime doffed his cover and bent at the waist in a deep and most royal bow in gracious recognition of our audience.

"That was just about the best music I ever heard in my life," I said out of breath.

"I am pleased at your enjoyment," said the man. "I am Elishua B. Tombatu the Third, a Nubian from far away Egyptia, at your service," he said. "And this"—he gesticulated with a sweep of his hat—"is the Pot and Pan Theater, home of dynamic thespian performance, lectures, sermons, tales of travel and adventure. I also offer music of all kinds, and remedies for all ailments, as well as a compendium of handy items for home and hearth."

"Looks like a busted-up wagon to me," said Pine Top.

"You t-t-t-talk f-f-funny," added Cheese.

Elishua B. shook his head with no little consternation.

"So it is, my friend," he agreed, "and so I do."

I proceeded thenceforth with formal introductions all around, and everybody took a shot at saying howdy, except Tiptoe Sam who seemed to view Elishua B. with some suspicion. Sam had by now stopped dancing and had built a fire and was starting to stack rocks into little piles.

"What are you doin' out here all alone by yourself and all?" Pine Top wanted to know.

"I am a Berber of the range," said he, "a wanderer—a nomad, if you will. My business and celestial sojourns take me over much of this great land, from one end to another. My wagon, however, has broken an axle upon this rocky earth. I was on my way to a revival meeting north in the village called Tulsa, and I've been here alone for a week. I'm afraid my provisions are beginning to become meager."

"You must be runnin' out of food too," observed Pine Top.

"Yes, that I am," said Elishua B., smiling warmly.

I figure Elishua B. is a good fellow, a gentleman for whom one should give a hand, seeing as he is a man of the cloth of some kind and a dynamic individual of entertainment and played "Sweet Beckoning Sue" so amazingly well and all. So I powwow with the others and among us we decide to help old Elishua B. fix his wagon if we can.

Near after an hour and fifty gallons of sweat among us, we manage to lift and roll the clanking, clonking, jiggly-jangly, wiggly buggy to a pile of boulders where we can perch her and get a better look at the underside of the problem. Elishua B. is by no means idle, expending easily double the energetic effort to secure the means of his transport and livelihood. Pine Top crawls beneath the wagon first to have a look, and then me, then Cheese, then Sam. Sam doesn't know much about wagons or things on wheels in general, but he wants to look underneath on account of he doesn't want to miss anything that might be of interest.

After much of the argument and disagreement that comes

among men akin on a common project without mutual experience, we finally land on the idea to shore that axle up with pot lids, nails, and pieces of metal of lesser importance from other parts of the wagon. And in spite of ourselves and after about half a day's hard labor, me, Pine Top McGee, Cheese Dinkle, Elishua B. Tombatu the Third, and Tiptoe Sam the hunchbacked Apache, get that wagon rolling just about like new when we're done.

Elishua B. is mightily impressed, and he gives us many fancy thanks to which we respond with an appropriate number of you're welcomes.

That night, we had us a wing-ding.

Before a big chip fire and under a fat yellow moon, Elishua B. got to telling us of his life on the revival, music, magic, medicine, pot-and-pan road. He tells us tales of robust, large-breasted, wild-lovin' women with skin as smooth as chocolate he had known in Egyptia, and he spins yarns of mysterious Nubian customs in places that nobody can pronounce even after he tells us how to pronounce them.

He breaks out a couple of bottles of what he calls his special Miracle Tonic, and we all drink some on account of we want to ward off any unforeseen trail ailments. We find that Elishua B.'s Miracle Tonic has more kick to it than a barrelful of your finest Coffin Varnish. And it tastes better too. Out comes the jerky, and we heat up some coffee and put some of that miraculous medicine in our tin cups and drink it with the coffee and sugar. Before you know it, we're all crazy drunk and singing, and I'm hugging Cheese like he's my best friend in the world, Pine Top is crying with sentimental happiness, Sam is dancing around, and we're all listening to Elishua B. play his echophone. Soon, before we know it, we all just drop to the ground dead asleep right where we sing.

Without really knowing it, that night it became a foregone conclusion that Elishua B. Tombatu the Third, the man from far-off Egyptia, would be traveling on with us in search of the mysterious stones of color.

Chapter 7.

SAM DISAPPEARS

We woke late that next day splayed all over the camp, all of us with a throbbing and a thumping headwise that made us a good bit cranky. Cheese was complaining about having to make breakfast all the time, and so rather than listen to him bellyache, I put Pine Top in charge of the coffee and bacon. We roused Elishua B. by wiggling his wagon on its springs, and me and Cheese and Pine Top were starting to eat when we noticed that Tiptoe Sam weren't nowhere around for his biscuit. Neither was his teepee present, nor his gear bags, nor his dancing noise. He simply was no place around.

Just then, an explosive shout comes from within the wagon of Elishua B.

"Blast that savage!" he hollers. "Blast him!"

Elishua B. bursts out from inside his wagon in flannel long johns, carrying on colorfully in a language that I've never heard before. It sounded to me almost like an ancient curse of some kind with many hard, rolling consonants and grunts in it.

"Someone stole ten bottles of my Miracle Tonic," wailed Elishua B.

"Take her easy," I said. "Take her easy there, Elishua B."

I squatted down in the dirt thinking, why would Sam do

such a thing? Why would Sam steal a load of Elishua B.'s Miracle Tonic and leave us alone here on the plain? Without Sam, we had no idea where to find the treasure. Maybe Sam was of a different mind under the influence of Elishua B.'s tonic? After all, it was as good as any Popskull available. Perhaps once its effects had faded, Sam would come to his senses and return?

"There's only one thing we can do, men," I said after considerable consideration. "We've got to follow Sam, try to track him."

"We g-g-g-gonna track him down an' k-k-k-kill him?" said Cheese with some hopefulness in his voice.

"We can't kill him," blurted Pine Top. "Sam's the only one knows the way to the treasure."

"Now you boys listen to me," I said with some irritation. "We ain't killin' nobody. Sam's our friend. A strange one, I'll give you that, but I get the feeling he wouldn't have done this thing without good reason. His travois drag trail is easy enough to follow, ain't it? The earth is soft and readable."

Pine Top and I examined the ground around and found Sam's trail easily enough. His travois left a wide drag mark behind him as deep and easy to follow as a road. Sam would have known that.

And Sam was heading west.

"We're headed west," I said with all the due conviction of a proper trail boss.

And hence we hitched Elishua B.'s wagon to his big horse, broke camp, loaded up, reined our horses and mule, and started to ride. We were traveling easier, seeing as most of our gear was now packed aboard the wagon. Fair exchange I figured for having Elishua B. along with us, and he had no objection to the intrusion of our meager gear into his mobile abode.

We had covered about four miles following Sam's bag-dragging when Pine Top discovered an empty bottle of Elishua B.'s Miracle Tonic in the dirt. Several miles farther along, we

THEY CALL ME NOONER

found another. From then on, Sam's trail got to meandering in a most confusing configuration: first westward, then southward, then northeast, then looping westward again. Sam was obviously losing his keen sense of direction, and if he was knocking away the Miracle Tonic, he probably was losing most of his other senses too.

As we continued along, the sky started to take on the wicked hue of pewter, and then, before you knew it, it unloaded. A hard, unforgiving storm came, the kind you enjoy on the plain when you least want to. We found shelter beneath some cedars and hunkered down to wait it out. For three days the rain fell, scouring any trace of Sam's trail from the earth.

And as the sky raged with lightning and thunder and pouring rain, we powwowed dry and warm and close in Elishua B.'s wagon. We were right smack in the middle of that storm, and at times the lightning came so close that the claps of the following thunder shook our little wagon shelter to its springs. The hair on our heads stood straight up at times, and all of us experienced curious tingling sensations in our extremities, even to the tender tips of our very dinguses.

Our host, Elisha B., seemed happy at our close company, and he didn't seem to mind the constant complaint and the potent stink of Cheese. Pine Top managed to fold and wedge his large frame into a nearly convenient configuration partially under the wagon seat, but it was a tight fit for four hefty men in that little wagon, no doubt about it. Pretty much everywhere you moved there was a man's leg in the way or a foot or a shoulder or a noggin or an arm or some such other appendage in your face at one time or another.

Elishua B. lit incense and candles that produced sweet smells to counteract the odor of sweaty men in tight quarters. He produced trinkets and baubles from faraway places that he bestowed upon each of us. He gave me a fine silvery ring rendered to resemble what he called a scarab, which I was to learn is a big beetle of some kind. The ring was inset with a glassy lava rock that made it smooth and pretty to look at. It was a ring, Elishua B. explained, that had come from the tomb of a wrapped-up old priest in Egyptia, and he told me that the ring would provide me luck to draw upon in the near future. And, as this tale will reveal, it certainly did.

And as we waited for the storm to subside, Elishua B. began to engage and amaze us once again with tales of his many adventures. His skills at elocution were impressive, and he was always pleased for any opportunity to unravel his vast and exotic yardage in colorful and descriptive fashion. He told us of the ancients in Egyptia who used to gut their dead and then bundle them up in broadcloth like packages. He spoke of tombs of ancient kings he had seen, places with statues the size of mountains all painted up fancy and decorated in real gold and turquoise. He spoke of buildings made of piles of gigantic rocks stacked to the heavens with finished triangle planes as smooth as glass that pointed to the sky. He told us that the ancients stuck them human dead body packages deep under these big piles of rocks to protect them so they might carry clean into the next world.

Right off the bat, it seemed to me that those ancient folks didn't have a whole lot more common sense than most folks do today. But I didn't say anything because the rhythm and the sincerity and the eloquent nature of Elishua B.'s voice and character were enlightening and impossible to deny.

Elishua B. also entertained us with queer songs in languages from strange places. He spoke of what he called the connective and transportive powers of music and enjoined us to include ourselves in his performances by banging on pans and singing aloud. He even played "Sweet Beckoning Sue" for me a few times on his echophone upon request. Elishua B. spoke as a preacher might. He spoke of the value of friendship and kindness and virtue, and how these three things can make a man's predestined, overall shitty life nearly bearable. He spoke of how the prejudices and stoogery of humankind put each and every one of us, and even the world itself, in peril on a most regular basis. There was plenty to ponder when Elishua B. had the floor, and ponder we did.

And then, three days later, the rain gave up the ghost. The sun rose clear on a blue and crisp rain-rinsed morning. And it was time for us to continue our search for Sam.

So off we rode once again.

I can laugh now, I guess. Thinking back on it, if you ever told me beforehand that I was going to be looking for a crazy, hunchbacked Apache with a skin full of Miracle Tonic, carrying a bag of rattlesnakes in hostile territory and dragging along a circus wagon besides, I'd have told you to take a running poke at a rolling doughnut. But that's the way it was, true as blue. And, as they tend to do in such unlikely circumstances, things were bound to get a whole lot worse before they got much better, as you'll likely see.

Chapter 8.

AMBUSHED BY THE ROID BROTHERS!

I guess it was about day five in our search for Sam, and looking back on it, we were all pretty careless. Me in particular.

Here we were just riding along, paying attention to the dirt to pick up Sam's trail again and not watching around us to see that we were working our way into the middle of a ravine ridge with towering rock on either side of us that spelled ambush.

And sure enough, just as we were in the middle of that ravine, a bullet kicked up some dirt next to Shithead. Shithead got riled, rose up on his hinds, and, as was his habit when he was skittered, dropped himself a hefty range muffin. I managed to stay on the goosey steed and keep him in check, but a report of more gunfire spooked him further and away I tumbled. Bullets peppered the ground around me as I flew runnin' to my feet.

Pine Top was off his horse fast and hit the ground running too, moving with surprising agility for a man of his girth and altitude. The two of us dove for cover behind a boulder and squinted up either side of the ridge, letting loose with return fire at nothing we could see. Elishua B. courageously dove headfirst into his wagon and emerged pronto with a huge plunger blunderbuss. It was an impressively robust and intimidating weapon but not at its most effective against hidden snipers.

"What's h-h-happnin'?" yelled Cheese, but he didn't have much chance to find out on account of his head busted open like a watermelon as a tumbling bullet cracked his forehead wide. He somersaulted gracefully backward off his poor spooked mule and landed headfirst into mud.

Meantime I've taken to running zigzaggy, looking for more cover, and the gunfire ain't layin' off. Then a fire explodes in my noggin as I guess a bullet zings me. It feels like somebody clogged me with a dogleg. I'm facedown and passin' out in the dirt, and the last thing I remember is feeling dirt going up my nose as I'm trying to remember how to keep breathing.

After this there's a lot of empty time, and the next thing I hear is a lot of wicked laughin'. I wrestle open my eyelids and don't much like what I see.

It's the goddam Roid brothers: Floyd, Lloyd, Boyd, and Roy. They're looking down on me and laughing like the dumbass idjits they are. They are the cruelest, meanest, dumbest, ugliest, sage sadist Indian-hunting nut sacks that ever walked upright like men. The Roids call themselves Indian hunters and have made a reputation and a living doing so, but in truth they're just an inbred bunch who get their jollies engaging in violent undertakings of a most vicious and perverse nature. Now that the Comanche have consolidated their power up to the north and most of the plains Indians are starving half to death, the Roids make their living digging up Kiowa burying grounds to make buttons out of the bones—among other industries of which I ain't likely to record here in consideration for those of a lesser constitution.

And now they've got us—that being me, Pine Top, and Elishua B.—trussed up like branding-line calves, and Floyd and Lloyd Roid are giggling like ninnies and poking at us with their boots.

"Howdy there, Nooner," says Floyd Roid cheerily.

"Hello, Floyd," I say, "you hairy, maggoty, horse-ball-licking, sheep-buggering shitbag."

Floyd titters upon receipt of my greeting. He is the oldest of the Roid brothers, built like a cannonball. He has long clumps of filthy black hair growing thick and long from every part of his body, including his ears, his knuckles, his nose, and probably even the tip of his tiny pecker. In spite of his formidable hairiness and compact form, Floyd has the unsettling demeanor of a little girl and is just the other side of insane.

"Hee-hee," he giggles. Then he leans over me and lets loose with a splurt of tobacco juice that catches me on the head. "Oh my," he says, pointlessly.

Then I see Boyd Roid, who wipes gingerly at his ear with a checkerboard handkerchief, looking down upon me with formidable malice. Boyd wears a tattered Confederate uniform with the insignia torn away, a smashed-up Confederate cap, and shiny spurred jackboots that he is known to polish for hours on end.

He's got a sore spot for me, Boyd Roid does, because the last time we met we got into an argument about a night lady he saw fit to punch around, and I rammed a jackknife as far as I could into his ear to discourage his behavior. I left him for dead, and obviously that was a mistake.

"Well, well," says Boyd, his bad ear swollen purple and infected and still seeping. "Nooner, Nooner, Nooner, Nooner. Betcha didn't 'spect to see *me* again, didja, you son of a bitch."

"Nope," I say. "Then again one don't expect to get the runs either but danged if it don't happen."

Boyd considers this observation but doesn't comprehend its wisdom, so he kicks me hard in the gut instead. I fold up like a pill bug, clutching my stomach with bound hands, huffing for air.

"We're gonna have us some real fun now, you bastard," he informs me.

"Brothers, good brothers," I hear Elishua B. say, in his gentle and reasonable tone. "Please…"

"Shut yer goddam mouth," growls Lloyd Roid, wringing a tent stake in his hand. Lloyd is the second youngest Roid—as crazy as a two-legged tarantula, as dangerous as a dynamite stick with a quarter-inch fuse, and as sinewy as a hangman's rope. His face looks all off-kilter, Lloyd's does, on account of his daddy dropped him down a mine shaft for fun when he was a baby.

"Why's he talkin'?" squeals Lloyd to nobody. "Didn't we hang the last one downwise to keep him from talkin'? Why you talkin'? Anybody *ask* you tuh start talkin'? Why's he talkin'? Tell him tuh stop talkin'. I don't want to hear this sombitch talkin', I swear to God." Lloyd walked over to Elishua B. and booted him hard in the head. "There goddam it. I jes' guess you ain't gonna be talkin' now, are you? Ain't talkin' now, is he?"

"Hee-hee, hee-hee," giggles cannonball Floyd in his awful little-girl way, and when he's done with his hilarity, he covers up one nostril with a dirty finger and empties his nose on me.

"Jesus howdy," I said.

I strained my neck over my bindings and looked over my shoulder at Pine Top. The big man was trussed up good too, his face distorted in pain as he cupped bound hands over what appeared to be a big black hole in his chest. He glanced over at me and shook his head.

"I'm shot," he said simply, "and my tooth hurts."

Suddenly, every sound in that ridge just seemed to die away, and the voice of Roy Roid came over us like a hot blast of desert wind.

"Long time no see, Nooner, yesss?" says he.

Roy Roid. The most dangerous of the horrible Roid brothers. If there is anyone who walks the face of this earth who can strike both a fearful respect and a sickening loathing into someone just by looking at him, Roy is that anyone. Roy's face is a pocked, pink oval with tiny chiseled features and a mean, thin-lipped mouth. He wears a clean flannel nightshirt, dungarees, and chaps. As he approaches me, I can see the remnants of shaving cream behind his ears and smell the suggestion of sweet toilet water on him. He's shaved close and wears a neatly brushed range cover, with cold hazel eyes that look flat and empty in spite of the fact that he's grinning. He toys with something in his hands.

The other Roid brothers clear the way for him, and I can see that what Roy holds in his hands is a razor, a glinting barber's straight razor with a blue edge that swings from a finely carved bone handle. Roy flips the blade open so I can see it and then slaps it shut into the hasp with confident, frying-pan–sized hands, his fingernails hard and yellow as horn. I've always marveled at Roy's hands. I've never seen a pair as hard or as powerful.

He pops that blade open again and strokes it with a nail, and the blade pings like a bell. Then he carefully slices a sliver of callous from the inside of his palm with the blade.

"Thought I'd wait and see you in hell, Roy," I tell him.

"You ain't easy to kill," Roy responds quietly.

"Easy as any man," I reply. "Just stop my heart, you son of a bitch."

"All in good time," he says. "First we've got us something to talk about, yesss? We heard us a little rumor in

Hunkerville, Nooner. A little rumor that me and my brothers here figured might stand a little exploration. Yesss?"

"No kidding," I say.

"Yesss," he whispers. "Yes we did."

And he knocks off my hat, grabs me by the hair, and lifts me with an amazing strength to a sitting position, looking into my eyes with a dead and empty expression. Then he presses his blade ever so soft onto my cheek and, in a smooth, almost loving motion, sweeps it down. The blade is so sharp I don't even know I'm cut until I see drops of blood popping up on my poncho and feel the heat of blood on my face. Roy runs a finger over my face and then licks the digit.

"You cut me, Roy," I say. "I don't like to be cut."

"Yesss," he says absently. "We heard something interesting, Nooner. In Hunkerville. Something very interesting. A bartender, wasn't it, boys? Wasn't it a bartender we were talking to?"

"That's right, Roy," says Boyd, daubing at his ear.

"Yes indeedy. A snooty barkeeper he was," says the hysterical one called Lloyd.

"Hee-hee," giggles cannonball Floyd. "He *was* a barkeeper. *Was* a barkeeper. Ain't gonna be barkeepin' much no more with no fingers left."

"You see, Nooner, me and the boys went down to meet an old friend of ours in Hunkerville," continues Roy quietly. "A man named Ed Looger. He ran a livery stable there. We found him dead. Murdered. And we also heard that a man named Dade Nooner happened to have been in town at precisely the time of his death. Funny, yes?"

"Hilarious," I said. "I'm barely controlling the hilarity that wracks my body."

"The rumor," continued Roy, "is that you and some cowboys and some crazy Indian have set out looking for a treasure. Now you know how me and the boys here love Comanche. Don't we, boys? We admire their culture so very much. And we know of their many fascinating legends too. Yes?"

"We love 'em dead is how we love 'em," suggested Lloyd.

"There wouldn't be any truth to this here rumor that we heard about, would there, Nooner?" Roy asked gently.

"Roy, Roy, Roy, Roy," I said. "You poor, dumb, twisted turd."

Roy, undisturbed, continued playing with his razor, flipping it open, closed, open, closed in his big hands and pinging the blade. Then he laughed. "Does that mean you aren't of a mind to clear up this rumor for us?" he asked.

"Suppose you tell me something first, Roy," I said.

Roy grinned wider, his lips stretching to reveal small, pointy teeth. "And what might that be?"

I looked him straight and hard in the eye. "You still get that bitty peter of yours going by strangling whores and then wearin' their underpants?"

Roy's mouth gets small, and his features compress. A vein pops out blue on his forehead, and his face reddens. Then he takes a couple of fast swipes at my face with the razor. I feel heat on my face that comes from being cut deep, and blood runs in rivulets like hot soup down over my shoulders, splattering the ground all around me. He's cut me bad this time.

Lloyd Roid jumps in then, excited at the sight of new blood. "That's it; kill him, Roy. Kill him. Kill that son of a bitch. Lookit what he done to Boyd. I say kill him, I really do. Who cares if'n you like underpants?" Lloyd is jumping in the air and wringing his sinewy hands together in a sickening display of crazy bloodlust.

Boyd Roid, his ear seeping, punches Lloyd aside. "You shut your goddam face, Lloyd!" says Boyd. "It ain't fair, Roy. That son of a bitch done stabbed me in my ear. If there's any killin' to be done, I oughta be the one what does it."

"Shut up, all of you," Roy said gently.

"But it ain't *fair*," whimpered Boyd.

Roy turned from me, and in a quick and economical motion, he swung a big paw and punched his brother Lloyd flat in the side of the head, catching him completely unawares, knocking him over and onto his butt in the mud. Then he kicked out with a big boot and caught Boyd square in the cojones basket, and Boyd's eyes bugged out as he bent in two halves, clutching at himself and tumbling slowly to the ground.

"Lloyd, Boyd," said Roy, softly chiding, "if you two don't shut your mouths and quit, the next town we visit will have a pig in it for you."

"Pig?" says Lloyd, lying in the dirt, rubbing his head. "Pig? Aw c'mon, Roy. No pig."

"Shut up then," says Roy. "Or pig."

And indeed, all the brothers shut up pronto. Roy's pig reference escaped me, but whatever its meaning, the suggestion of a waiting pig in the next town was somehow so absolutely abhorrent that it silenced even the repulsive Roid brothers.

Roy turned his attention back to me. "I can see you haven't changed much, Nooner," he said, grabbing me by the hair again and giving me that cold eyeball.

"I haven't changed in weeks," I blurted, spitting blood.

"So, what say you be smart," said Roy. "Tell me what I want to know, and you can spare the lives of yourself and Pine Top over there and that pan-handling preacher or whoever he is."

I take a long look at Pine Top, who is hurting pretty bad and looking pale by now with his wound and all. Then I take a look at Elishua B., who is lying unconscious in the dirt. I realize that we're all in for the hard road now, anyway you cut it. I also don't know what Roy thinks I know, and if I tell what I don't know, sure enough he's going to kill us all. If I tell him what I *do* know, he'll kill us. So I make the choice that seems the one least likely to discharge his murderous instincts.

"Go ahead and kill us, you son of a bitch," I told him. "And kill the preacher and that big old dumbass cowboy too if you've a mind to. You can torture me and make buttons out of my bones if you want, but I know what I know, and you sick bastards are going to have to keep us alive if you want a piece of what we're lookin' for."

Chapter 9.

THEM BEANS

The sun dropped. The Roid brothers leave us be so they can powwow. Elishua B. is still passed out in the dirt. Pine Top has passed in and out a couple of times from his bullet wound, and the blood is so caked up on my face and neck that I crackle when I turn my head. I can almost put my tongue through one cheek.

The Roids get to talking. I can't make out what they're saying, but they're carrying on in earnest, and I know I've managed to buy a little time.

Roy Roid, being the greedy son of a bitch he is, has decided to give the situation some deep consideration. I've given him pause, which is not an easy thing to do with a man of Roy Roid's evil immediacy.

Roy knows I'm good on my word because we've crossed paths many times before. My hatred of him and his lunatic brothers is enough to carry me over into the otherworld if it has to. He knows I ain't scared to die.

The Roid brothers decide to amuse themselves awhile by going through Elishua B.'s wagon, stealing what's left of our food, throwing our gear into the dirt, and taking whatever else they think they might want. They also help themselves to some of Elishua B.'s tonic.

Roy tells Lloyd and Floyd to cook up some of our chow while they think on the problem at hand, and during their supper, the smell is driving me and my appetite a little crazy.

Lloyd staggers over to us, tonic happy. "We got us some beans," he taunts, holding his plate in front of me and slopping food into his face. "Hot, good beans." Then he walks over to Pine Top. "Soft, cooked tasty beans," says Lloyd. "Hey, these danged beans is mighty good, Pine Top, all cooked and soft, and you can eat a whole lot of these here beans if'n you tell us about that there treasure gold."

Pine Top is conscious. And he's hungry, I know, because he's hungry all the time. And right about now I'm sure he's as hungry as a man can get being wounded and all and needing his proper nourishment. But he holds.

"I had beans before," Pine Top says hoarsely. "Beans ain't no big deal."

"Sure ya have, sure ya have," says Lloyd, leaning over him close. "But not beans like this. See, these here are soft little beans slurpin' in molasses. We got lotsa these here beans, too. We eat these beans up, me and my brothers. Sometimes ya can eat 'em one at a time, and sometimes ya can eat 'em in a big spoon all at once. Like this."

Lloyd picks up a big steaming heap of beans, puts that big wooden spoon into his lopsided mouth, and starts slurping and making other groaning noises as if he was eating the most glorious foodstuff on earth.

Pine Top, agitated, lets out a roar and rears up his two bound feet hard, catching Lloyd's plate with both legs and slamming it square into Lloyd's face, and danged if that old wooden spoon don't lodge deep down Lloyd's gullet, and them beans from his goddam plate fly everywhere and sprinkle in the dirt around us like some kind of bean rain.

"Eat them tasty beans like that then!" bellows Pine Top.

Lloyd drops his plate and takes to choking and dancing around and turning colors a man shouldn't turn. Then he hits the ground flat on his back, tugging on the handle of that wooden spoon, which is now well-rammed most of the way down his rotten, goddam gag hole.

Brother Floyd stops his giggling, runs over, and grabs ahold of that spoon with both hands and yanks and yanks, and finally he puts his boot on Lloyd's forehead and manages to pull the spoon out of Lloyd's throat along with stringers of goo that was down inside his brother.

Me and Elishua B. and Pine Top started laughing like crazy men. It made us all strong. "Cut me loose!" I yelled at Boyd with a sudden hysterical bravado. "Cut me loose and give me another jackknife, you pus-oozin' jackass, and I'll finish what I started!"

Well, needless to say, this incident got them brothers fairly riled. Boyd was all over me, punching and clubbing, and Floyd was whacking at Elishua B. with a poker for fun, while Roy stood and watched with his big hands on his hips and a look of consternation on his face. It was passing-out time for me again, what with the fresh beating I was receiving, but on the edges of gray, bloody, near-unconsciousness, I heard Roy's voice cutting through the pummeling.

"Hold it off!" he was shoutin'. "Hold it off, boys!" Then I heard two gunshots, and the Roids broke off us like flies shooed off a range patty. It got all quiet again in that ridge except maybe for the crackling of the campfire and the thumping of what was left of the blood in my veins. Then Roy's voice came again. I couldn't see him, but I could hear him in the night, his voice as cold and sharp and dangerous as that razor he carried.

"We wait, boys," Roy said. "We wait until first light and let the cold of the night work on these boys a while. Then we'll have us some good fun loosening their tongues when we're all good and rested and they're all the more tired and cold and hungry. Gives us all something to look forward to on the morrow. Yes, brothers?"

"Okay, Roy," said his siblings, with what I couldn't help but notice was some considerable disappointment in their tone.

They gave us a once-over, heckled and beat on us a little more for fun, and then checked the security of our bindings. Roy ended up bedding up in Elishua B.'s wagon while the other Roid brothers got around to wrapping themselves in blankets around the fire. That left me and Pine Top and Elishua B. unprotected in the cold of the night, bleeding and rattled and half beat to death to do battle with the longest night of our lives.

Chapter 10.

VENOMOUS VENGEANCE

The fire had burned nearly out, the embers casting a faint orange pall around the camp. The night was about halfway through and very cold and silent save for the snoring of the three fireside Roids, the occasional moaning of poor Pine Top, the mumbled prayers of Elishua B., and the chattering of my teeth.

I had found myself a dull rock and was making useless headway with it on the thick and greasy rope that bound my wrists. After a while I couldn't feel any sensation at all in my fingers, and I was worried about having frostbitten toes.

I knew I was going to die.

And then I thought I heard a sound in the night. A soft thump it was, so soft. And then there was a dragging sound, and then the almost imperceptible sound of what I took to be bare footfall on the earth. I heard another thumping sound and then another. And then I heard a sudden brittle hissing chorus of agitated rattles! It was rattlesnakes! Sounded like a dozen of 'em, maybe more!

The most god-awful, bloodcurdling screaming I ever heard or ever will hear in my life busted out among them fireside Roids. I was confused—half out of my mind from pain, exhaustion, and blood loss—but in the light, such as it was, I could make out the three of them Roid brothers as shadows suddenly on their feet jumping and dancing and caterwauling and pulling at themselves. Two of them broke out on a flat run, and I could hear their shrieking fade as they made distance. Roy Roid came flying out of the wagon at the commotion and was hollering, "What's going on?" and a muzzle flash of gunfire cut into the night after him, sending him reeling. In the flash of the blast I saw, or I thought I saw anyway, Roy Roid standing on the stanchion of the wagon wearing nothing but a pair of black, lacy lady underpanties. All of it seemed an impossibly wild apparition.

There is a rustling behind me, and I catch a big whiff of something like fresh-cut cedar. Suddenly my ropes fall slack.

"Sam!" I yell. "Sam, you're back!" And I am about as glad to see him as I ever thought I'd be to see a tiptoeing Apache hunchback.

Sam said nothing, moving swift and silent as a shadow, first to free Pine Top and then Elishua B. Then, without a sound, he disappeared back into the brush.

"Pine Top! Elishua B.!" I'm yelling. "Sam's back! It's Sam!"

"Sam?" mumbled Pine Top vacantly. "Sam!"

I climbed to my feet and hobbled as well as I could over to the fire to look down on the Roid brother who'd been left behind. It was Boyd, rolling around, terrorized in the dirt. I felt something slither by my leg and jumped back with a hoarse shriek. Writhing over and hanging off Boyd and fanging into him again and again were about some of the most riled and rattling rattlesnakes I'd ever seen. All of them, I realized, from Tiptoe Sam's bag.

Elishua B. appeared at my side, looking down at the rumpled, wrestling, shrieking form of Boyd Roid.

"I'm bit, I'm *bit*!" moaned Boyd, already starting to fever up. "Do somethin'," he cried. And he *was* bit; that was for certain. There were about a dozen sets of hideous red and welting fang marks dribbling blood on his face and neck alone.

"You're bit all right, you son of a bitch," I said. "You're about as bit as a man can get."

Boyd started to jerk around, his arms flailing spastically as the venom worked its way through him. Elishua B. couldn't watch the spectacle, turning his face away. But goddam it, I watched. I sure as hell watched. I watched until Boyd Roid stopped his kicking. I watched until he let out his last filthy goddam breath. I watched until he was as still and as dead as a turd. I had left him for dead once, and I sure the hell wasn't going to make that mistake again. Death is rarely pretty, I remember thinking, but on a man like Boyd Roid, it was a lovely thing to see indeed.

"A man does best when he sees things through to completion," I murmured quietly to myself, reminded of Elishua B.'s observation.

Sam came running behind me, holding his big hemp bag open in a kind of hysterical ministration. "Get snakes!" he shouted. "Get snakes; put 'em back!"

Obediently I held the bag open, and one by one Sam picked up them angry rattlers off the ground and chucked them back into his bag. One of them was stubborn, still stuck on Boyd's neck, and as Sam pulled it loose, it nicked Sam one.

"Sam," I yelled. "You're bit!"

"Ha! No more poison," Sam said. "Poison used up on these assholes. Little poison makes Sam stronger anyway."

I gave Sam back his bag and then threw a couple of pieces of wood on the fire to stoke it for better light. I rolled Boyd's contorted body off his blanket.

By now Pine Top was on his feet, sweating and tottering and out of breath, and I could tell that he wasn't doing real good.

"I got me a bullet in me," he explained.

"Sit down by the fire and quit wobblin'," I commanded. I turned my attention to Tiptoe Sam. "Sam! Did you get Roy? Did you get the one in the wagon?"

"Buckshot," Sam said, shrugging. "Winged him."

I ran over to the wagon and circled carefully behind it looking for Roy. There was blood spilled here and there, but no Roy. Gone. Roy was gone.

But now he was alone. Shot up some. On the run. And wearing only a pair of scanty, black lady lace underduds.

Things were lookin' up.

Chapter 11.

BULLET-HOLE MEDICINE

The campfire was going strong by now, and I returned to it. Sam stood beside it holding his wiggling snake hemp bag in his arms, looking down on Pine Top with a drawn expression of deep concern. It was the first time I'd seen him in such bemused condition. In most things, Sam seemed to find a sort of amusement, but not now. I patted him on the hump and told him many thanks for killing the Roid brothers, disregarding for the moment that he was the reason we were all cut up and in this lousy predicament in the first place.

Sam wouldn't be comforted. He looked up at me and touched my bloody, scarred face with a soft hand; then he turned away from me so I couldn't see his face.

"What about the other evil men?" Elishua B. wanted to know.

"I reckon the only one we have to worry about anymore is Roy," I said. "And he ain't exactly dressed for travel."

We looked down on Pine Top who was shuddering violently now, his arms wrapped around him in a bear hug, the sweat running down in streaks on his face. I tucked a blanket tight around him.

"There, there, old boy," I said. "There you go now."

"Colors. Colors, Nooner," he told me. "Stones of many

colors." And then Pine Top turned over onto his side and threw up.

"The Pine Tree man sees the other side," observed Sam to the fire.

"We need to bring him back to this side," I said. "Do you know any bullet-hole medicine, Sam?"

"Yes," said Sam. "Much."

"Good," I said. "I'm going to need your help. Elishua B., see if you can round up a couple of good-sized bowie knives and a bottle of your tonic. There should be a couple of riding gloves in my saddlebags if the Roids didn't steal 'em. Get 'em."

Elishua B. went off to do the tasks.

I ripped open Pine Top's shirt to expose his wound. It was an angry hollow above his right teat and about as big around as an apple—greenish on the outside and inflamed, bloody, and black on the inside. A reeking infection from the wound had already begun to take hold.

I had never seen infection occur so quickly in a gunshot wound. The only thing I could figure was that maybe the Roid brothers had gone to the trouble to dip their bullets into some vile substance to accelerate the process. It would be just their style.

"Here, Nooner, the Miracle Tonic," said Elishua B., tossing me a bottle.

I uncorked it and took a long pull from it; then I pressed the bottle to Pine Top's lips and upended it. Pine Top gulped, choked, and splurted. A lot of the juice ran down the sides of his face, but I think I managed to get about half the bottle down him. Then I poured the rest of the bottle on Pine Top's wound, which made him howl like a hound.

"I'm cold, Nooner," gasped the big man when his howlin' was through. "I'm real cold. I got a bad tooth." Then he started singing as the Miracle Tonic started to take hold. "Sweet beckonin' Sue..." As he sang, he tossed his head and rolled his big body from side to side. "Sweet beckonin' Sue, beckoned me awa-a-ay from the one that was true-u-ue..."

"Take her easy on the vocals, big man," I told him. "We're gonna get to work on you here some soon. Sam, get us some water to put on the boil."

Sam knotted up his bag, tossed it to the ground, and ran away, rummaging through the wagon for a bucket. Elishua B. produced two large knives he had recovered from his wagon. I set them on a flat rock at the edge of the campfire, the blades exposed to the flames.

Sam was back in a few minutes with a bucket full of water and a handful of leaves and root.

"These are good," said Sam. He set about arranging the bucket of water over the fire.

Pine Top by this time had quit his singing and had started whimpering like a baby, his big old hands grabbing at the ground and the side of his face pressing into the earth. "Long ways from home," he was saying, delirious-like. "Long, long, long ways from home..."

Sam crouched and began carefully feeding kindling to the flames nearest the knives. Together we blew on the fire, encouraging a great heat, and pretty soon the blades of those knives began to glow. I dropped the riding gloves into the boiling water for a minute or two and then pulled them out with a stick to cool. I wrung them out and pulled them on hot over my hands.

We rolled Pine Top to his back. "Now hold him down," I told the men. "You got to hold him down good, boys. I mean it. Put your knees on his shoulders and press down on him with all your weight. Use your whole body, Elishua B., Sam, you got to hold his legs." I swallowed dryly, knowing the worst was yet to come.

I positioned myself in a straddle over Pine Top's chest, pulled one of the hot knives from the fire, took a deep breath, and pushed that glowing bowie knife deep into his festering wound.

Pine Top's flesh sizzled and spattered like bacon, and he started screaming—screaming something horrible—with his body jerking and fighting. Smoke was coming up, and as I tried to cut away the dead flesh, I could smell the stink of his skin and hair and flesh as it burned. I started to gag and almost passed out; then I steeled myself and continued with the cutting. Elishua B. had his full weight on Pine Top's shoulders, but Pine Top was a very powerful man, all wrestling and shrieking and kicking. Elishua B. and Sam were hanging on for all they were worth and pressing down on the big man for dear life.

"Hold him down! Hold him still goddammit!"

Pine Top somehow got his hands around Elishua B.'s neck and was squeezing, and Elishua B. was now above ground and at the same time trying to bounce Pine Top down. Pine Top was screaming until his voice turned sore and ragged and he couldn't hardly scream no more. Then all of a sudden Pine Top's eyes glazed over and rolled up into his head. Then his body went limp, and he thumped flat to the ground like the toppling tree he was named after.

I really get to work now with the hot knife, ripping and cutting the cooking dead chest meat away and digging deep and making the least mess of things that I can. Sam holds a burning piece of kindling over the work so I can see better. I'm sweating like a fire-eater, and Elishua B. can't watch any more. He looks away, leans over, and throws up.

Fortunately for Pine Top, his chest muscle is tough and sinewy with gristle, and the bullet didn't get much past the bone. Just a couple inches. I clear away most of the dead meat I have cut away, throwing it into the fire, and finally I get down to where I can see the bullet, all silvery at the bottom of the bloody mess I've made. Then I work the point of that bowie under it and out it pops. I give the bullet to Sam, who then rinses out Pine Top's meat crater with cups of the boiling water. Sam also pours some of the water over my gloved hands, now slick with blood.

I took the other knife from the fire, almost white-hot now, and started to work the blade around and deep into the wound. There was more sizzling and spattering, and Pine Top's body stiffened again; then he shivered to a terrifying and absolute stillness.

Elishua B. daubed at poor Pine Top's forehead with a wet kerchief, and Sam took to smearing some of them leaves and root he found into the wound. I took another chug of Elishua B.'s tonic and poured a little more over the whole bloody mess just for good measure, then bandaged it all with a piece of clean folded linen, and tied it all tight around his chest.

When finished, I pulled back and looked over Pine Top's body. He was the color of shale, his breathing was very shallow, and for some reason he looked a lot smaller. I threw the blood-soaked riding gloves spattering into the fire.

"Better say a prayer for him, Elishua B.," I said. "Make it a long one and touch on all the gods you can. He's going to need all the help he can get. I ain't no goddam doctor."

Elishua B. hung his head and got to mumbling something appropriate, and I just sat there trembling by the waning fire, not thinking about anything—not having the energy to think. After a while, I realized that it was the twilight of morning, and seeing the light of the new day, I started to weep some. I was just about shot to hell, I guess. Embarrassed, exhausted, and wounded, I stumbled away and gently lay on a blanket where I fell into the sleep of the near dying.

Chapter 12.

BULLETPROOF

Iremember waking that next day, realizing hazily that Sam was working on me. He had cleaned me up with boiled cloth and then taken up the careful application to my razor-hacked face of a foul-smelling poultice of his manufacture. It was the pungent smell and the sting of the poultice that awakened me. I looked up at him in a daze, and he smiled down at me gently. He patted my shoulder, and I passed out again.

It was a couple of days before Pine Top came around. When he did, he was still some delirious and in pain and stiff enough that he couldn't hardly move. But at least he came awake, and we were all glad of it. All we could do now was try to make him as comfortable as we could and lick our wounds until we felt fit enough to get moving.

We were worn and mighty hungry but had fortuitously doubled our provisions. Elishua B. prepared for us a miraculous meal of biscuits, jerky, ham, and coffee. And yes, even beans—hot, steaming beans smothered in molasses. Still, beans never quite tasted as good to me ever again.

Tiptoe Sam was the only one who didn't eat much. Most

of the time all he ever needed was a biscuit or two to get by. During this time of our recovery, he took to wandering on the outskirts of the camp, looking for Roy.

Besides the food surplus that the Roids had left behind, we found ourselves stocked with seven more guns, including a couple of Colts and a Winchester rifle, plenty of rounds, some sticks of dynamite, some knives, pots, utensils, four sets of boots, four saddles, and four more horses. I've always said that death may be emotionally grim for some, but somehow always profitable for somebody or another who happens to have managed to stay over here on this side of dead.

After we eat that big meal, Sam squats down by his teepee and gets to tinkering with something, and pretty soon we all come to find that Sam is working on decorating a strip of buffalo thong he has cut from his coat. He has adorned the strip of hide with a couple of feathers and some beads he carved out of sticks and has tied that bullet we pulled out of Pine Top's chest right in the middle. With much typical dancing and noisemaking ceremony, Sam approaches Pine Top and ties the whole who-dee-dee around his neck.

"What's this all about yer doin', Sam?" Pine Top wants to know.

Sam grins his three-toother. "Pine Top man will now be protected from bullet holes," he explains.

"No? Yer joshin'," says Pine Top. "Ya mean I'm bulletproof?"

Sam nods.

"Well, what do you know?" says Pine Top in wonder. "Hey, Nooner! I'm bulletproof now! Sam says I'm bulletproof!"

I nodded. "Good for you then, Pine Top. When we get to riding, you're up front from now on, and you can draw the fire. We'll watch the slugs bounce right the hell off."

Pine Top smiled, and I noticed that his eyes had some of their shine back. "You betcha I will," he said proudly. "You betcha." And he took to resting, pleased, under a tree and noodling with his bullet.

Me and Elishua B. got to tidying the camp and taking a full and proper inventory of our overall gear, food, and firepower.

The next day Elishua B. and me rode out in search of panty-clad Roy. We didn't find him, but we did detect the tracks of that lone, barefoot, pantied son of a bitch, and he seemed to be headed west. After a while we discovered, too, the remains of the two other Roid brothers splayed out about a quarter mile from one another. They were as dead as Custer, these two, and the buzzards had already been having themselves a feast, picking and chewing and ripping at the Roids' soft parts. Finally, I thought, these two Roid brothers have found something they're good for.

When we got back to the edge of camp many hours later, we discovered that Sam and Pine Top had gone out and recovered the body of Cheese Dinkle from the ravine, where we were all first assaulted by the Roid brothers. Together, they had buried him properly beneath a mound of rocks in a cool and shady spot. Sam and Pine Top were the both of them standing over Cheese's grave looking solemn when we rode in upon them. Elishua B. and I dismounted, uncovered, and took us a spot near the grave.

"I knew Cheese Dinkle pretty good," observed Pine Top by way of a eulogy, "and Cheese Dinkle wasn't a very happy man. And because he wasn't very happy, he didn't make nobody else very happy either. I don't know much, but I don't know if you can blame a man for not being happy if he don't have much to be happy about in the first place. But I think ol' Cheese...well, ol' Cheese...he did the best he could smelling the way he did."

"Amen," we all said.

Chapter 13.

A FRESH SPIN

That night Sam got around to telling us, after a fashion, where he had gone when he had deserted us just a couple of short weeks previous. Rather than scribing the conversation exactly as it occurred, I figure to summarize here due to the choppy and singularly laconic nature of conversation with Sam. Trying to get multiple words per sentence from Sam when he doesn't want to talk is akin to convincing a skunk to hand over a chicken egg. A vast repetitiveness of inquiry is required in any attempt to extract information from the likes of Tiptoe Sam. Hence, I have scribed here the gist of what I eventually managed to pry from Sam's lips in a style that them fancy scribin' types in them nickel cowboy books refer to as literary compression.

It seemed that he, that being Sam, decided to abandon us for a quick journey west to take council with an old friend of his, a Cherokee chief, into whose proximity we had travelled. The chief's name was Saxquamethaka or Sackademaka or some such permutation, I can't quite remember. Sam, being the impulsive hombre he is, made this journey impromptu, alone, and without the courtesy of consultation or notice.

Sam was hoping that perhaps his old chief friend might have news concerning the whereabouts of his old gal,

Wickey-Wickey. Sam stole some of Elishua B.'s bottles of Miracle Tonic as a sort of exchange incentive for information, with the intention of repaying Elishua B. Tombatu with some carved beads or a rattler at a later date. Unfortunately for Sam, he became enamored of the tonic on the trail and lost his direction along the way, just as I had guessed. But eventually, Sam recovered his bearings and finally made the company of the old chief, whatever the hell his name was.

Together Sam and the old chief powwowed, exchanging news and war stories, and Sam was to learn that Wickey-Wickey had indeed been last seen in a big Comanche encampment up north.

When I was through with my efforts at information extraction from Tiptoe Sam, the old warrior still looked as though he had something on his mind.

"Something else you wish to discuss at length, Sam?" I said, poking fun at him in my own style of humor, not expecting to get much more out of him.

"There was a golden-haired woman at the Cherokee camp," Sam said with some somber reluctance.

"A golden-haired woman?" I said.

"White golden woman named Hat," confirmed Sam. "Says she knows Nooner."

"Hatty?" I said, incredulous, my heart doing double time. "Sam, are you telling me my girl Hatty is out west in a Cherokee camp?"

Sam shrugged. "Hat woman say that she is looking for Nooner Boss. She is taken by Cherokee chief. Hat woman stays with chief for a time, but says that Nooner cannot spurn her love any longer. Woman small but has good chest pillows big like water bladders and a heart as big as a mountain."

"Goddam, that would be Hatty," I said to myself.

Well, this just put a whole fresh spin on things: Hatty. Alone in a Cherokee camp. Looking for me.

I walked away from the others then, picked up a stick to

chew on, and got to thinking on this news. And, after chewing up a good coupla more sticks and considering, I walked back to the men, my mind made up.

"Boys," I said, "Hatty is a woman who has been following me from the ends of the earth on and off for near to five years. I figure I got to find her and get her out of that Cherokee camp before she gets herself into trouble. I figure I'll bring her back here, and we'll continue on our way to the treasure."

Pine Top and Elishua B. mumbled some in disapproval.

"Women ain't no good on no long trip," fretted Pine Top. "Besides," he added, "they overall make me nervous."

"Hatty makes me nervous too, Pine Top," I told him. "But it won't take me long to fetch her. Right, Sam?"

Sam shrugged. "It will take as long as it takes," he said. "Umma."

"Well, in the time it takes for me to make the trip, you men ought to be about healed up enough to ride. Right, Pine Top?" I said. "Right?"

"I don't know 'bout no woman though," Pine Top mumbled.

"The pursuit of love often has many detours," Elishua B. warned.

"Well, boys," I said, a little cranky now, "I don't know if I'd call it the pursuit of love." I realize now, of course, that I was lying to myself as much as to them. But at that moment I had done all the considering on this I intended to do. "That treasure ain't going no place," I said. "And Hatty ain't all that sensible and liable to get her dumb self killed."

Sam looked at me, his face creased deep in secret amusement.

Jesus howdy, I thought. Half the time I'm trying to get away from Hatty; the other half I'm chasing her down to save her ass from her own self. Some gals just won't take no for an answer.

Chapter 14.

CHIEF WHATEVER THE HELL HIS NAME IS

I saddled up Shithead there and then, warning the men to stay put and keep their eyeballs peeled for old Roy just in case he showed up. I stocked up on a few days' provisions, said some goodbyes, and then, with directions provided by Sam, headed west toward the Cherokee camp of Chief Sasqueetchaka or Sakajaweeakkadoo, or whatever the hell his name was.

As I ride I get to thinking about Hatty—thinking about her warm, ripe body; her firm, full haunches rising lovely from her long and tender legs. I get to thinking of her pretty face and her golden hair, soft and fine, and the way her body used to feel all hot and bothered wrapped around underneath and bucking and kicking, and the two of us laughing and raising a hoot and having a hell of a time in general. I feel a familiar shifting in my dungarees and realize that I haven't had a good one in about three long months or maybe even more, nor even allowed myself the luxury of thinking about women. This makes me ride a good bit faster, although with considerable discomfort.

In the middle of the third day of riding, I see some smoke billowing out of a little clearing surrounded by scrub and realize that I have reached the outskirts of a tiny and very shabby excuse for an Indian camp.

Carefully I make my way to a rise where I can take a look-see over the whole outfit. There's about ten or fifteen pretty poop-poor Indian men down there, along with a few maidens and naked babies running around scraggly teepees. Don't see no sign of Hatty.

I'm not sure if these Cherokee are going to be friendly or not, but I have to take my chances. I'm hoping maybe Tiptoe Sam has mentioned me in his visit and these poor folk aren't of a mind to try to shoot me on general principle. Anyhow, I figure it takes more than ten or fifteen Indians just over dog weight and a bunch of naked babies to bring me down.

I ride higher on the hillock and let out with a whoop. Then I wave, making a sign with my hands that I hope the Cherokee take for a peaceful one. The children scatter, and the Indian maidens run around gathering them up. The braves of the camp glare up at me, jabbering among themselves and pointing, arguing about what to do.

Finally, two braves mount a couple of sorry-looking soup-bones and ride slow up the hillock to meet me. They are quite noticeably armed. I keep my hands in clear view at all times on account of Cherokee tend to be a bit skittish around strange pale folk.

The first brave is hardly a brave at all; in fact, he isn't much more than a boy. But the proud way he rides and points a rifle at me you'd think he was wearing a medal on his chest. The second is a brave closer to my own age, kind of funny looking, and as skinny as a fence post with big puffy cheeks that look like apples and eyes that are too close together. Both are naked except for little stringed doodads with pouches in the front to hold themselves in, and both are adorned with feather and bone.

They stop about ten feet from me, brandishing their weapons and giving me a careful eyeball.

"They call me Nooner," I said. "I come in peace in search of my friend, the great Chief...uh...Sasquawatchicka." I could have kicked myself then and there because I realized that I still hadn't fully memorized whatever the hell the chief's name was.

The two braves looked at one another curiously, then back at me.

"*Who* do you seek?" said the older brave, speaking with a dignity that belied his pitiful condition.

"Chief Suchasquweeka?" I tried.

The older brave shook his head. "No Chief Suchasquweeka here," he said.

"Howsabout a Chief Sackawacakawally?"

"No," said the brave.

"Well," I said, highly embarrassed by now, "you *do* got a chief around here *somewhere,* don'tcha?"

"Yes," said the older brave.

"Sunkawallhachi?" I tried, hoping that maybe this brave might take pity on me sometime soon and let me off the hook.

Eventually, with reluctance, he did. "You mean Chief Sasquametchakuwan."

"That would be who I mean," I said. "And what is your name, brave warrior?" I asked the young one.

The little brave looked at me and sneered.

"That would be Little Bear Foot," said the big one. "And I am called Deer Leaping Over the Pond. What is it you want with our chief?"

"I need to speak with him and ask him about a friend of mine. A woman friend with golden hair."

"Ha," said Deer.

"Ha?" I said.

"Woman you seek has been here. Woman has fine bosom big like boulders."

"That would be Hatty," I said. "Please tell your chief I'm a friend of Tiptoe Sam and that I've come for his counsel."

Deer turned and spoke to Little Bear Foot in Injun. They carried on for a moment, seeming to argue about something. Finally they turned their attention back to me. "Give us your guns," Deer said.

Not having much choice, I handed over my Peacemakers and sawed-off. Then I followed the two braves down the slope and into the camp.

As we made our way along, I got the tough eye from the other braves. Indian Maidens peeked out of their tents to take a gander too. Some of them screeched and ducked back inside. I think it was the razor gashes on my face that frightened them.

Finally we stopped before a large teepee inscribed with strange symbols perched in the middle of the camp. It was surrounded by rocks all piled around in tidy heaps, lots of things made out of sticks, and the usual skinny critters that Indians tend to keep around to eat when times are lean, which for these folk looked like a good deal of the time.

Deer disappeared into the teepee and then came out.

"Chief Sasquametchakuwan will see you," he said. "But he is angry to be awakened from comfy nap."

I dismounted Shithead and handed Deer the reins. "Take care of my horse, Shithead," I said. "And be careful. He bites."

Deer's expression clouded. "I am Deer Leaping Over the Pond," he said angrily. "Not Shithead."

"Yes, Deer," I sighed.

I entered the teepee and there sat old Chief Whatever the Hell His Name Was on a pile of horse blankets. He was very old, but his eyes were sharp and they peered from under a thickly ridged brow that gave him a noble demeanor. His face was wrinkled as crumpled paper, and his hair, long and loose, was as silver as a new coin.

"They call me Nooner, and I come in peace," I said.

"White rider's name is mud, and full of bullshit," croaked the old chief. "Preacher?"

"Do I look like a preacher, Chief?" I said.

He studied me.

"What is wrong with your face?" he wanted to know.

"Razor," I said.

The old chief laughed. "White rider should be more careful shaving. Or grow a beard," he said.

"I am in search of a golden-haired white woman with breasts like water bladders," I said.

Chief Whatever the Hell His Name Was sighed. "Who isn't?" he said.

"My friend Tiptoe Sam the Hunchbacked Apache was here," I told him. "A week back."

"Hunchbacked men always have weak backs," observed the chief.

"That's not what I meant," I said.

"White men never say what they mean," the chief pointed out, not without some accuracy.

I took a breather and tried again. "Sam told me that he saw the golden-haired woman. With you. In this camp."

The old chief nodded. "Sam was here, yes. Sam is a good friend. He has much magic in his old bones. He brought me strange whiskey in bottles to drink."

"And the golden woman?"

The chief nodded. "Yes, she was here. She left in the night. Took Chief's finest horse."

"She's gone?"

"Very much," sighed the chief.

"Oh fine," I said, much bemused. "Ain't that just goddam fine."

"The woman tires of sitting in teepee all day," mused the chief, more to himself than anything. "Chief likes the golden woman here. She is good to look upon. But she tires of sitting in teepee all day. Boring in teepee all day. Golden woman told me that she looks for white rider, Nooner. And you are the Nooner?"

"I am," I said.

Then we didn't say anything for a time.

"Lucky Nooner," he finally said.

"Sometimes," I said.

Then, again, we didn't say anything for a time.

"Well," I said to break the quiet, "I guess I should be shoving off to find her then."

The chief seemed suddenly distressed. "Is that all?" he asked.

"Well, yes," I replied.

"Nothing to trade? Meat? Whiskey? Fur? Beads? Beaver?"

"Nope," I said. "Sorry."

"Need advice? Hear old Indian tale? Learn a rain dance?"

"No thanks, Chief," I said. "I don't have the time. Got to get moving."

The chief sighed again sadly. "Day shot to hell," he said. "Tell Sam howdy for Chief. Tell him thanks for the coming. Sam is a friend of mine with much magic in his old bones."

"I will, Chief," I said. "And maybe we'll meet again someday."

"Maybe," he said. "Maybe not. Chief is very old. People too poor. White poachers take all the life from the hills, and there is no hunting."

"I know," I said, feeling a flush of shame.

"Chief may die soon. Boring in teepee all day. Chief is seeing strange visions in the night."

"Visions?" I said.

"Chief left teepee late in forenight to do a thing. In the night Chief sees a vision of a man with large hands running through camp in small woman underthing." The chief sighed again. "Chief is seeing strange visions in the night. Chief not well. Boring in teepee all day."

Chapter 15.

HORSE SENSE

I told the chief that the man in the unmentionables he thought he saw in the night was not a delusion, but a true and dangerous killer named Roy. Upon receiving this news, the chief was much relieved if not a little confused.

"What does this mean when a man wears a fancy lady underthing?" the chief asked.

"I don't know, Chief," I said. "But if you see this man again, take it from me, kill him dead and don't think twice about it. I've known him for a long time, and he's as mean and bloodthirsty as a man can be."

The chief brightened. "I'll send braves to search," he said, pleased at the prospect of having something to do.

"Any idea which direction the golden-haired woman went?" I asked.

"Eastway," said the chief. "She took the Chief's best horse. Need help tracking?"

"No, I don't think so." I rose. "I'm obliged to you, Chief, but I must go. Goodbye, and many thanks for the help."

I flapped open the teepee and took Shithead from Deer Leaping Over the Pond, who was standing just outside with Little Bear Foot. The two braves escorted me back up the hill from whence I had come, and once we were what they considered a safe distance from the camp, they gave me back my guns, and I was on my way.

And back I rode, wondering where it was that I had missed Hatty. I rode hunkered down and meandered, looking for some sign of her on the earth, but none could I find.

A day passed. Nothing. And another. Nothing. The nights were lonely and getting colder. I was worried plenty, and Shithead was cantankerous and skittish.

Here I feel I must insert something on this whole cowboy mythology about man and horse. Much hoo-ha has been made of this relationship. There are those who will carry on with wild and romantic exaggeration regarding the clever and protective qualities of a mount. They'll tell you magnificent stories that will bring a tear to your eye about a horse's enduring loyalty and overall heroic nature. But I'm here to tell you that horses have got to be the dumbest, meanest, most self-absorbed company a thinking man can have. They're short on brains and lousy on conversation, but they have just enough cunning to make life a living hell for a man. They know that your very survival often depends on them, and they take every opportunity to remind you of the fact by injuring, terrifying, and degrading you whenever possible.

Now to take the horse's side for a moment, I guess I might be testy if somebody hammered nails in my feet and rode around on my back all day long in the heat, but a horse's cunning has a maliciousness and deviltry all its own. And none of this will you ever read about in those cowboy nickel books.

I've had lots of horses, and not one of them would ever swim out in a river to save me if I was drowning, or wait patiently for my return if it was unfettered, or be coaxed to jump a big ravine with me on its back to escape murderous desperados. Hell no. Every horse I ever had would take a chunk out of me whenever it had the chance, give me a good kick in the ass if I wasn't looking, or buck me off hard and step on me to boot at the first sign of danger. I've known a half dozen good men who got their skulls busted in and their brains kicked out by their loyal, heroic, loving mounts.

Shithead was no different; that is to say, most of the time no better or worse than any of the others. But experience has taught me a hard lesson—I've got the scars to prove it—and because of this, no way in hell would I ever bestow upon any horse of mine a noble or sentimental handle.

Shithead's latest infraction occurred when I was trying to bed down after that third day of hard riding and no Hatty. I had set up my little camp, unrolled my bedroll, made a little fire and such, and had walked a ways in my long johns to a stream nearby to wash up and pot some water for coffee. I was returning when I found that Shithead had somehow worked loose of his tether. He stood not too far away, watching me with that mean defiance in his eyes peculiar to the species.

Slowly I moved toward him, speaking quietly to soothe him, and just as I got to within reach of his bridle, he cantered away. I moved toward him again, slowly, carefully, and again, just as I got to within grabbing distance, he skipped away—not too far—just enough to show me his keen sense of distance. Well, this went on and on for some time, until we were maybe a half mile away from the camp. I knew that if I gave up, Shithead might decide to run off, and that would be the sum end of my capability for transport. So I played his game, my annoyance building considerable.

Well, sure enough, I was moving in on him again, by this time seething and cursing and as crazy mad as a man can be in his underthings in the middle of nowhere while trying to maintain his composure, when off Shithead went, this time at a fast gallop, disappearing into the dust.

Well, that was it, I figured. Shithead was gone. I was henceforward on foot. So I trudged dejectedly back to the camp. But when I got there, who do I see but that goddam conniving horse just standing there looking as innocent as you please and chewing on some grass as if nothing had happened. Shithead had made a wide circle and come back.

Needless to say, I was giddy to see him, and was in the process of reevaluating my over-all contempt for horseflesh, when I noticed that Shithead had done his full day's worth of horse business all over my bedroll, clothes, and hat.

Chapter 16.

DANDY DAN

The next day I rode some more, aiming toward the encampment of my compadres. I had pretty much given up hope of finding Hatty. As I rode along, the terrain was painfully the same, mostly miles and miles of not a damn thing in sight to see.

To pass the time I got to thinking about the first time I met Hatty. We had met in the little town of Dimplerood, a small ways from Tumbletown and a good bit a ways from Crooked Leg, to give you an idea if you need to get your bearings. I was killing time playing at cards in a saloon there in Dimplerood, and Hatty was standing around looking bored and available in her pretty lace dress. I bought her a whiskey, and she accepted it and put it away fierce and in a hurry.

The moment I set eyes on her I knew she was something special, just like you know there's something special about a cool fall morning when there's still frost on the squash or when you come upon a nice flow of good water that runs clear even if it's in a dusty ravine. Besides her fleshy body configuration, which she makes immediately noticeable and powerfully desirable, Hatty has a pugnacious demeanor and low tolerance for cowboys who might try a grab at her without providing proper compensation in the primary. She can throw a fast haymaker that comes out of nowhere—I've seen it—and she knows exactly where to find the notch in a cowboy's jaw to knock a man unconscious in order to rifle pockets and acquire currency or new belongings in safety.

Hatty has a gravelly voice, too, that I like quite a token, and the woman talks and talks and talks. She likes to talk, and she talks about things that she might like to do and she talks about things she might like to wear someday or maybe some place she'd like to go or some cake she had once or a goddam recipe she wants to try or some hat she had that she liked a lot because it had blue feathers on it or whatever the hell it is that she wants to talk about. Her conversational direction is a type that takes many puzzling detours along its way, and her dialogue seems to bounce from subject to subject without rhyme, reason, or resolution. To be honest, I only ever half-listen to what Hatty is saying at any given time because to follow her conversational line with any semblance of attention will eventually carry an hombre to a state of deep confusion, befuddlement, and distress.

Yet all this somehow makes Hatty one of the most desirable women I've ever known, profound titties and fine round bottom notwithstanding. Her prolific gab suggests to me a woman of some considerable intelligence well beyond her gender. And maybe most importantly, Hatty's demeanor offers a constant and unflagging hopefulness and cheer that propounds the possibly that good things lie ahead, even in what I've found a reliably shitty world. For a suspicious roustabout such as myself, this is a most welcome feature of the woman indeed.

As I was thinking of these things, a small valley opened below me, and from this vantage I spotted a curious cloud of dust. Under that dust cloud I could make out the tiny figure of a man perched on a rock in the middle of a dry creek bed. Shithead and I moved down the rise to investigate.

It was an old man down there, and from the looks of him

he was a prospector, what with digging tools and shovels and what-all spread around him in the dirt. A couple of weary mules were tied to a withered tree. The man had a look of impatience on his prickly sunburned face. A corncob pipe was jammed upside down between his dry lips, and in his hands he shook a dented gold-panning pan full of dirt. He slowly scooped up some more dirt from the creek bed in that pan, shook it around a bit, studied it carefully, shook his head, and then dumped it out and scooped again. I watched him do this for a while, then rode up to earshot.

"Howdy, old-timer," I said.

But he didn't answer me.

"I say *howdy*!" I said again.

Goddam if he still didn't answer.

"Ain't too friendly, are ya?" I said.

He still didn't say nothing.

"Well goddam. You deaf or just stupid?"

"I ain't neither," the old man snapped all of a sudden. "My name is Dandy Dan, as if it's any of your goddam business."

"Ain't much on conversation then either, I take it," I suggested.

"Ain't feelin' chatty," he said.

"Well, what are you doing out here all alone?"

"What's it look like I'm frickin' doin'?" he yapped.

"Looks like you're wasting your time," I said.

"My time, ain't it?" he said.

He had a point.

"Right enough," I said. "But you got a lot to learn about if you think you're panning for gold."

"What do you frickin' know about it?"

"I know enough that you can't pan for gold in no dry creek bed," I said.

Dandy Dan studied me then. Then he barked,

"Wouldn't be trying to jump my claim, wouldja?"

I snorted. "Claim? You call this here dusty creek bed a claim?"

"Just a matter of time," he said, digging again with his pan.

"I guess nobody told you that you've got to have water to pan for gold?"

"I got me a water bag," said Dandy Dan.

"I mean you got to have water flowing in the creek to pan for gold," I said.

"You do? What's the point of that? A man'd get wet to the bone in a hurry now, wouldn't he?"

"So he would," I said.

The old man glared at me some more. Then he said, "You goddam young punchers think you know every goddam thing, don'tcha?" And he scooped, studied his dirt, dumped it out making a cloud, and then scooped again. "I seen Custer," he said, more to himself than anybody. "I killed outlaws. I been on Injun campaigns all around this territory. I been hung twice, branded once. See?" He held out his forearm, and there was a mean circular scar with an "S" burned there. "I rode with the frickin' Rangers. I killed me a goddam grizzly bear with a stick. I was raised by wolves. I had me a silk coat that a Chinese give me. I know a goddam thing or two. Goddam young punchers think they can just ride on up and know everything."

"You ain't seen a blonde-headed woman riding in these parts, have you?" I said.

"Pah," he said. "I seen her. Pretty, she was. Titties the size of baby pigs."

I felt my heart flutter in my chest. "That would be her," I said. "When was that?"

"Couple few days ago," he said. "Rode right on past here."

"Which way?"

"That way yonder," said the crazy old prick, and he held his pan aloft to point east.

I pulled on Shithead's reins, hardly able to conceal my excitement.

"How did she look? I mean...did she look all right?"

"Goddam right she looked all right!" the old man leered. "Bout as pretty as a water mirage."

"Well thanks," I said. "I wish you luck, old man."

The old prospector got vicious again. "Luck ain't got nothin' to do with it," he yipped. "Goddam young punchers think they know it all. Don't know nothin' about patience. Just a matter of goddam time," he said. Then he scooped, studied his dirt, dumped, scooped again, and dumped again. "You might want to learn a thing about patience, you goddam young puncher. There's a whole lot to be said about patience nowadays."

"I'll keep that in mind, Dandy Dan," I said under my breath.

Then I rode off in my own cloud of dust, leaving that crabby old-timer with his dented-up pan, his cloud of dust, his upside-down corncob pipe, and about all the goddam fricking patience I could possibly stand.

He watched me angrily as I rode away until I couldn't see him anymore.

Chapter 17.

POOLS

Still not a sign of Hatty anyplace. But at least I was again hopeful from the babble of old prospector Dandy Dan who, in spite of his considerable experience, didn't seem to know a damn thing about prospecting proper.

I rode and rode many more miles, getting all the more tired and all the more thirsty until I spotted a small, lush patch of land—a piece of quiet and comfort gathered against a large unlikely run of gentle green. The place was sheltered by sycamores, cedars, and willows, which seemed to have had no business being there.

Shithead was as tired as I was, and just as thirsty, so I put him up to water at a clear little pool born of a spring that burbled from a mouth of smooth white granite. The spring turned into a gently flowing little creek that trickled and then widened to collect into several clear, deep pools. It was an unusually peaceful place, rich and quiet, and quite unlike the surrounding range.

So peaceful and kind was this spot that I decided to take a doze. The sound of the water trickling over the smooth rocks rockabyed me into a relaxation I hadn't known in some time. I snoozed undisturbed for several hours and woke up soft and easy to the sound of birds in the trees. A breeze moved the leaves around me with a sound like the rustling of crisp bedsheets.

I decided to take a swim. I dropped my duds buck naked to take a little sip and dip in the biggest of the pools. Easing into the coolness of the water, I floated half asleep, letting a gentle current carry me along from one pool to another. I floated down to a place where the stream was dammed by beavers. Big cedars hung over the water here giving shade and cool, and I could see trout fishes flashing among polished pebbles at the bottom of the water. The pool was deep enough to where I could stand upright. The water came up to my neck, and I could feel the stones mossy and slick underfoot.

And as I stood there in the deep cool water, I leaned my arms onto a fallen log and took a look around the other side of the beaver dam, and there, just beyond where the creek began to head south, I saw Hatty.

Naked as I am she was, her hair tied up on her head in a golden knot. She was knee deep and splashing water over herself while humming soft without a care in the world. I couldn't help but marvel at how beautiful she was in her secret nakedness, and for some reason this moment still sticks in my mind as one of the most tender I've ever known.

I watched her for a while, my heart aching in my chest. Then, under cover of the trees, I snuck out on the bank and quietly circled around over to her.

"Howdy, lady," I said, poking my head from behind a tree.

Hatty started and looked up, covering herself with her arms. Then, seeing that it was me, she lowered her modesty and shook her head. She'd always been pretty proud of that body of hers.

"My Lord," I said. "If you ain't the most beautiful thing I ever saw."

She looked me up and down, smiling, her face flushed and brilliant. And then suddenly, her expression changed to one of anger.

"You son of a bitch," she said. "Beautiful, am I? I guess I ain't beautiful enough for you to stick around, am I?"

"Hatty..." I said.

"You big dumbass, Dade Nooner," she said. "I been following your sorry trail since Waco, and you figure you can leave me behind just because you think you can ride a horse better'n me? And I'm ridin' and ridin' all over this goddam plain and can't even get the dirt outta my toes. Did you ever try to get the dirty outta your toes, Dade? On account of it sticks to your fingers and then you wipe 'em on your dress, and then what do you get? I'll tell you what you get. You get dirt on your dress is what you get. And this here's my nice dress that Aunt Aggie made me outta old curtains and a feedbag. You remember Aunt Aggie?"

"Whoa! Hatty! Listen, I..."

"Jack crap, Dade," she said. "You listen to me, you sneakin' poke." She splashed water at me with her arms in kind of a silly display. "You think you can leave me behind like a bad goddam pony all the time? After all them promises you made? You break my heart is what you do, on a regular basis. On account of you think you got something important to do every time and then off you go, just hit the trail, don't even say goodbye to nobody or nothin'? You're about one mean, discourteous son of a bitch."

"Hatty...I was just..."

"You was just nothin'!" She waded on up over to me, and then her expression took on a fearful look as she got a gander at me. "Oh my good Lord in heaven, Dade," she exclaimed. "What happened to your pretty face?"

"I'm all right, Hatty," I said sheepishly. "Just a scratch or two."

"Oh my good Lord in heaven," she said again, and her fist went to her mouth. "What happened? Some son of a bitch done hurt you? What happened, Dade? What happened?"

"Hatty. It ain't nothin'..."

Then she got angry again. "Every goddam time I catch up with you you're worst off than before," she said.

"Seems to me I caught up with you just now," I said, "if I remember correctly."

She stood there in the water, goose bumps over her skin, her tummy heaving from the cool of the water. "Well, don't that tell you somethin', Dade Nooner? You keep runnin' from me but end up findin' me yourself?"

She had herself a point, but I wasn't exactly sure what it was.

"Don't that tell you something, Dade?" she said again. "If you was to settle down and quit riding away from me on them adventures of yourn, I could take care of you and...and you wouldn't have to be on no trail no more, and you wouldn't get all beat up and cut up and drunked up and shot at all the time. I could make you soup and biscuits," she said. "I make real good soup with carrots in it and maybe some beans, and it would be kind of like a chili almost, except it would be a nice soup. Or maybe I could just make chili after all if I had some chili powder and some pepper." Her eyes started to tear up. "What are you runnin' from me for, Dade? Why you runnin'?"

"I ain't runnin'," I said stubborn. "I just ain't got no stake to settle with, Hatty. We been through this. I'm a lone wolf. I gotta be on the move until I get us a stake and get to a place I want to be."

She sneered. "The place you'd like to be. Where is that place, Dade? Where is that goddam place you'd like to be? You'd like to think you know," she said, "but there ain't never gonna be no place you'd like to be. Ever. You ain't gonna be a big, tough ramblin' puncher all your life, you know. You ramble and ramble and ramble, and you gonna ramble right into a big hole in the dirt is where you gonna ramble, and that looks to me like the place you'd like to be, whether you'd like to be there in a big hole in the dirt or not."

"Maybe I will. Maybe I won't," I said, because I didn't quite know what to say.

She stuck her pretty dimpled chin out to me. "I'm strong, Dade," she said. "A healthy good woman. Look at me." And I did. "I could bear you strong sons. I can cook and I can build us a home and I can wash up, and I look fine when I'm full washed. My toes won't have dirt in 'em neither. Maybe a little daughter while we're at it. And we can be at it all you like, Dade. You always like bein' at it most the time; I know you do. I like bein' at it too. We can be at it all the time, whenever we want to be."

I looked away. But she wouldn't be denied. We had both been through hell for a while. I looked back at her. She held her naked body out, her hands on her soft hips, her admirable body thrust forward.

"It's good enough for me," I said. "But Hatty, it just ain't... timely. There's things a man's got to do. Things I got to see, you know...and I got to see as much of it as I can before I decide to take up fixing fences and busting up goddam dirt clods and raising a bunch of booger-pickin' kids forever until I die of bein' bored."

She wrapped her arms around herself then, her eyes downcast, her breasts swelling and falling with her breathing, her face flushed with anger and frustration.

"Well, I'm goin' with you," she finally said. "I'm goin' with you, I'm goin' with you, I'm goin' with you. Until you get over this lone-wolf business."

"Oh no you ain't," I said, holding my hands up in the air. "Oh no you ain't, Hatty. Trail ain't no place for a woman."

She ignored me, gathering her hair in her hands and wringing it out. Then she arched her neck until she was looking up into the cedar branches above. "I been ridin' and shootin' my way over the trail following you around off and on for near to five years," she said. "And by myself, by the way, you dumbass."

She turned then and walked toward the shore. And I

watched her as she moved, soft, fair, and beautiful.

"Maybe..." I said, chasing her down, moving through the water, splashing. I caught up with her and put my hands on her shoulders from behind.

"Maybe nothing," she said.

But she turned and I pulled her to me close, and she let me. I felt her body cool and soft and molded against me. I held her tight then and kissed her, and she let me do that too without hittin' me on the jaw.

"Dade...you..." she whispered.

"Hatty...I..." I said.

I put my mouth on hers again, and she trembled. I held her as together we set that way down naked and gentle and easy onto that grassy bank near that clear water pool.

Chapter 18.

HATTY

We lay side by side on a horse blanket on the shore of the pool. Hatty spun a little yellow flower in her fingers, watching the water.

"Where you learn that little love trick you did just a minute ago?" she asked.

Actually I had learned that love trick from a gal named Sallie Teacups in Galveston, but I wasn't of a mind to tell Hatty that.

"I don't know what you mean," I lied, sweet as maple.

"I bet you learned it from some whore someplace," she said.

"And seems to me," I said, suddenly angry, "I've heard tell of your own sizeable love appetite with a trail bum or two."

Hatty rolled onto her front side, her breasts pressed flat and full into the earth, and I could see where the pine needles had stuck to her bottom. I could also see the little half-moon scar there where my horse Shithead once savaged her. All of a sudden her body was heaving, her hands on her face. She was crying, her elbows in the needles.

"Awww, Hatty, goddammit," I said. "C'mon. Don't cry."

"A woman's got needs inside of 'em too, you know, you son of a bitch," she said. "And I shot more trail bums than I ever loved on. Besides, if you was around, I wouldn't need no other trail bum."

"It don't please me to hear you been with some other," I said. "It don't please me one bit."

"Well, I got news for you, Dade Nooner," Hatty said. "I'm riding with you from now on. I'll cook for you and I'll take care of you, so there ain't gonna be no need for no other no more ever again. How's that?"

I got up and stormed around, swinging my arms helplessly and being all angry and jealous and naked and no place to go and flustered and tryin' to clear my head of the cloud of confusion buildin' there. I remembered an old Chinese coolie once told me that lovin' a woman is like grabbin' a sword by the blade; you're gonna get cut both ways if you decide you're gonna grab it. I looked back at Hatty, and she was sitting there on that blanket Indian style now. She'd quit cryin' and was laughin' at me, laughin' like crazy, and the only thing I could figure was now that she had completely confusicated and pestered and skullduggered me, she was as happy as hell again. Go figure.

In my experience these women are the most confounding, bewildering creatures ever in any immediate area, capable of providing a man's greatest pleasures and his greatest miseries at their leisure and all at the very same time, too, if they've a mind to.

Chapter 19.

DINKY

Hatty found her clothes by the creek and got them on, and we found her horse, a strong paint. I was still runnin' 'round raw on account of my gear was upstream.

"That's some fine horse you stole," I told her.

"You met the chief?" she said.

"I met him trying to find you," I told her.

"He was good to me," she said. "The Comanche fed me and took care of me. I feel bad about stealing his animal, but it was the only decent horse they had in that little camp of theirs. I figured I was in for a lot of riding, and I didn't know how long it would take to find you."

"So you just go skipping into an Indian camp pretty as you please and steal their horses, and you ain't worried them braves are going to come after you? Ever think on that?"

Hatty giggled. "Them braves wouldn't scalp me," she said. "Some of them Indian maids might, but not them braves."

"Pretty dang sure of yourself, ain'tcha?" I said.

"Cherokee ain't mean natured, Dade. All their meanness been knocked out of 'em by them Roid brothers and that Captain Crook."

"Took all their buffalo and most of their dignity besides," I added.

"Yes," Hatty agreed.

"So how the hell did you know where to look for me in the first place, Hatty?" I asked.

She looked at me coyly. "A woman has her ways," she said.

"She does, does she?"

"Yes she does," she said. "You still ridin' that old, mean goddam horse, Shit for Brains?"

"Shithead. He ain't that old," I said. "But mean he is."

"Don't I know it," she said, patting herself on the bottom where Shithead left his mark.

I was still naked, and I walked beside as she rode. We worked our way along the creek bank and eventually to the spot where I had set up. But as we approached, I realized something was wrong. Shithead and all my belongings were gone.

"Jesus howdy!" I said.

"What?" said Hatty. "Dade?"

"Somebody done robbed me."

"You sure?"

"'Course I'm sure," I said.

And I started running around searching high and low in that little clearing under the shady trees for some trace of something left, but there was nothing there of mine behind to behold. And indeed I felt naked as a baby. All of my gear right down to my long john thompsons—gone.

"Ain't that just fine," I said. "No guns, no horse, no saddle..."

"No britches," added Hatty, and I noticed she was giggling a little. "Thievery don't seem to agree with your pecker either."

"I'd like to know what the hell is so funny."

"I can't help myself, Dade," she said, and she started laughing in earnest now. "You look so helpless and comical running around all mad and naked and your dingus all dinky like that."

"Well, goddam it, woman. You ain't making things any better."

"I'm sorry. I'm sorry, Dade," she said, but she was still just barely managing to control her laughter.

"Well, hell. Britches or no, we got to get back to the main camp," I said.

"Where's that?"

"A day or two due east. I got a handful of men waiting for me there."

"A day or two is a long time to be without your britches," she observed.

"You're telling me," I said.

"You walk around buck naked in this sun for two days, and you're liable to get a sunburn on them white buns of yours and your danglin' hat besides," she said. "And you're likely to freeze it all up at night too. In all that cold, your dangler might decide to just pull on up inside yourself and disappear most entirely from view."

She was starting to giggle again, and I was getting all the more testy.

"You better just quit that goddam laughing," I warned.

"I'm tryin', Dade; I'm tryin'," she said.

"Well goddammit," I said. "What's next? What in the hell blazes is coming next?"

Hatty started laughing again, and this time she was laughing so hard that the tears were coming up in her eyes. She reached into her saddlebag and held something out for me to see. And in spite of myself, I got to smiling, then grinning, and then finally I was laughing pretty good too.

Because, by God, now I knew what was next.

Chapter 20.

HATTY'S EXTRA DRESS

Hatty's extra dress was a dandy, a pretty blue with nice puffy shoulder lace and cut kind of low in the front. It fit me a little snuggy in the waist and was a little longer than I would have liked, but once I got used to it, I got to admit, it was real comfortable. I had a nice breezy feeling between my legs and on my dangler and my two amigos as I walked that I hadn't experienced before. And, without getting strange about it all, I could see why it is that ladies take to wearing dresses rather than britches most of the time.

Hatty had her namesake Cimarron revolver close at hand—she always carried that wood-handled Lightning that her daddy give her. He taught her how to shoot way back when she was just a little dust bug, so at least we had us some protective firepower, and she was a damn good shot, too, was my Hatty. We took turns riding that paint when my feet got sore, and we made lousy time, but we weren't in any big hurry anyway. Hatty couldn't stop laughing and making fun of me. I got her back plenty anyhow, goosing her when she wasn't looking and appreciating just having her around in general.

We loved on each other most of that first night and didn't get much sleep because of it, but it didn't matter because I felt about as satisfied as I had in a long time. A sliver of moon was out, and Hatty always looked her best when dressed only in the moonlight. She and I got the owls hooting and the coyotes howlin' along with us.

But all that time through the trip back, I also had that unsettling feeling you get when you know somebody's watchin' you. I hoped it was my imagination, but usually when I get this kind of notion there's something to it. I've learned that you got to trust your instincts. I didn't tell Hatty about it, but I'm pretty sure she felt it too.

Finally we made it back to the camp where Elishua B., Sam, and Pine Top were waiting. They were all three sitting around by the wagon playing cards for matches, looking bored as hell. Upon seeing me ride up wearin' that dress, Pine Top took to laughing real hard and slapping his leg, and Elishua B. smiled at me, too, but took care not to let too much of his amusement show. Sam walked up to me, looked me up and down. He shook his head and sighed. "White men are strange," he said in summary.

"Well, look it you," said Pine Top all hilarious. "We thought two lovely ladies was ridin' up to see us. I'd say you're a changed man, Nooner!"

I scowled at him. "Well, at the very least, it looks like you've got your laughing strength back, Pine Top," I said. "Boys, I want you all to meet Hatty. Hatty, meet the boys."

"Sam and I have met," said Hatty. "How do, Sam."

Sam nodded his Indian nod. "Hello, golden one," he said. He embraced Hatty, making sure to enjoy clutching a handful of her fine soft bottom in the exchange.

"Oh, Sam," said Hatty.

Sam's coat was flopping open all the time, and I couldn't help but notice that Hatty was admiring of Sam's big old red dingus that was always hanging out. Didn't bother me any because every gal I ever knew always liked looking at different danglers whenever they got the chance.

Pine Top strode up to Hatty, his big black hat in his hand.

"Uh, glad to meetcha. I'm Pine Top McGee," said Pine Top. And then, because he didn't know what else to say, he added, "I'm bulletproof."

"How do, Bulletproof Pine Top McGee," said Hatty. Pine Top turned as red as an uncooked prairie beet.

"I am very pleased to make your acquaintance. I am Elishua B. Tombatu the Third, a Nubian from Egyptia."

I noticed that Elishua B. had introduced himself proper and was careful not to leave anything out of his long and most impressive title. He kissed Hatty's hand.

Hatty did a curtsy and said, "Ain't you a fancy gentleman, then?"

And I'm not sure, but I think that Elishua B. turned the color of an uncooked prairie beet too. Hatty is so lovely to behold that most men turn the color of an uncooked prairie beet as a general rule.

"Anything happen while I was gone?" I asked.

"Whole lot of nothin'," said Pine Top in a doleful tone. "Thought maybe you run into Roy, on account of you was gone so long."

I looked at Hatty. "We might have," I said. "Somebody stole Shithead and the rest of my gear down to my boots as perhaps you can plainly see."

Hatty shivered. "Roy Roid?" she said with considerable apprehension.

"'Fraid so, Hatty," I said. "Hunchbacked Sam here killed the rest of them dirty Roid brothers, but Roy got away."

"Oh my Lord," said Hatty.

"Well, you needn't worry," I said. "There's five of us and only one of him. And we got his pants and all his firepower."

Pine Top walked up to me a little hangdog. "I didn't mean to be laughin' at you just now, Nooner," he said. "But you just look all funny with your big legs and your chest all hairy and hangin' outta that purty dress and all."

"Never mind it," I said. "Just let's get to the wagon and see

THEY CALL ME NOONER

if we can find some of Roy's clothes I can wear. Elishua B., I want you to find me a coupla the best pistols that we got. And load up that Winchester for me too. Sam, I need you to build us a good fire for supper, and then I want to take a scout look a quarter mile or so all around the camp. I don't want any more dang surprises with Hatty here."

"You boys hungry?" Hatty asked.

"I know I am," said Pine Top.

"Well, there's a surprise," I said. I patted Pine Top gently on the shoulder to let him know everything was all right.

"I'll make us a good supper," said Hatty, having studied the provisional situation and already busying herself with preparation. She was a hell of a cook, my Hatty.

"And after supper, I want you hombres to pack up and get ready to roll at first light," I said. "We've killed us enough time already. Tomorrow, boys, we're back in the treasure business. Ain't that right Sam?"

Sam looked up from the pile of sticks he was stacking and nodded. "Umma," he said.

Chapter 21.

PROPOSAL

Roy's clothes were a pretty tight fit. Actually, I would have preferred to keep wearing Hatty's dress if only for the sake of comfort, but what would the others have thought?

While the men were out and around doing odd jobs, Hatty and I sat together by the fire while a critter stew cooked.

"So what's this I'm hearing about a treasure?" she wanted to know.

"Well, we're going in search of a Comanche treasure, Hatty. Up north some."

"Oh really?" she said drily. "A Comanche treasure it is then."

"That's right."

"You're of a mind to steal a Comanche treasure."

"Yep."

Hatty stared at me, incredulous. "I don't suppose it matters that the Comanche happen to be the most ferocious tribe on the trail and would just as soon scalp any white man as first say howdy-do?"

"There is that," I said. "But hear me out. Did you notice that rock Sam wears around his neck?"

"I did," she said.

"Do you know what it is? It's a gold nugget, that's what.

And Pine Top says that Sam probably knows where there's a whole lot more of them just like it."

"Probably knows? Sam probably knows? Dade, you gone crazy? You're gonna ride into hostile Comanche territory because Sam says he probably knows where there might be a treasure?"

"He told me right where it is," I said.

"Sure he did."

"Well, he kinda did. In his roundabout way."

"Dade, don't it seem unlikely that Sam would betray an Indian nation for three white men?"

I thought on this a minute. "Why not?" I finally said.

"Well, what's in it for him?"

"He's looking for his lost woman, a Comanche gal he loved on some years ago. Wickey-Wickey he calls her. We told him we'd help him find her if he showed us where the treasure lies."

Hatty sighed. "Of all the ridiculous notions you've come up with, Dade Nooner. The Comanche are buffalo hunters not treasure hunters. Far and wide as I been, I never heard of no Comanche ever havin' no treasure."

"Legend has it that they lost it," I explained, "on account of Sam says he stole it."

Peeved, Hatty rose and slammed a big skillet on the fire pit.

"Well, howdy on a stick, Hatty!" I said. "What are you riled about now?"

"Didn't it ever occur to you that Apache Tippy-Toe Sam might just be havin' himself a little joke at your expense? Or that maybe he's just a teeny-tiny tetched in the head?"

"I suppose," I said sheepishly.

"Sometimes you ain't got the sense the Lord gave a horseshoe," she said.

"Well, Missy Know-It-All, if you think a minute," I shot back, "maybe you'd see that if we do get the treasure, just maybe I'll finally have that settlin' stake I been looking for all this goddam time." I guess I was starting to get pretty angry, and I suppose I shot off at the mouth before my brain was properly engaged.

Hatty stopped sulking and her expression softened. "You thinkin' about settlin'? Is that what you're sayin', Dade?"

"Well, I...I guess so. I been thinking on it; let me put it that way."

"Oh, Dade," Hatty said. And giggling with delight, she put her arms around my neck and, hugging me tight, kissed my face a bunch of times real good. "Does this mean we're engaged?" she shrieked.

"Well now don't jump the gun, Hatty," I said. "Let's not get ahead of ourselves. We haven't got to the treasure yet."

"But if we do...?"

"If we do, I'll make you a deal," I said. I can't quite believe that I was saying it, even though I was. "If we find that treasure...we'll get engaged."

"And then?"

I took a deep breath and saw my life unfold before me just like they say it does before you die.

"Maybe then...maybe then we'll homestead ourselves a piece of land somewheres and get ourselves married. Maybe now, you hear? We'll just have to see."

"Oh, Dade!" Hatty exclaimed, and she kissed me sloppy some more on the ear.

I remember thinking, Oh Lord, Dade, what have you done? What in the blazes have you done here, Dade Nooner, you big, dumb, clod-bustin' trail muffin?

Chapter 22.

COUNSEL WITH SAM

We got on at first light with hunchbacked Tiptoe Sam leading the way, dragging his stick travois as before. He was followed close behind by me and Hatty and Pine Top on our horses while Elishua B. took up the rear, riding in his tonic-laden, pot-and-pan clanking, multicolored theater wagon.

We traveled for many days, all without much incident. In fact, our progress seemed almost easy. We were moving mostly across open plains country and didn't have to worry much about bears or cats or wolves eating us. Hatty was traveling with a contented smile on her face. She was suddenly as intent on finding this Comanche treasure as were we.

Sam was leading the way, doing the scouting and tracking, and with his help we managed to keep our water up, and our provisions held up too. Hatty did the cooking, Elishua B. played his echophone at night for our entertainment, and Pine Top was almost all the way back to his old self from his bullet hole and even managed to shoot us an occasional critter to put in the pot. The weather was fine most of the way, except for the cold of night and a rainfall or two. Still, although the traveling was nearby enjoyable with Hatty so close, I still felt strangely uneasy.

Sam seemed bothered some too. He had become quiet,

less inclined to do his dance, and even once neglected to pick up a rattler that was sitting in the sun.

Late one clear cold night well into the journey, everyone was sacked—Hatty snug in the wagon, Elishua B. and Pine Top out soundly by a crackling fire. As usual, I couldn't sleep for I was lately kept awake by nightmares and skittishness. I decided to approach Sam's teepee to inquire as to our proximity to the treasure and his recent unusual disposition.

I stole from Hatty's arms and out of the wagon as quietly as I could and approached Sam's dwelling. I knocked as well as I suppose a man can on a teepee, then flapped it open, and poked my head in. It was the first time that I had ever ventured into Sam's domain. Sam was a man who liked his privacy.

A tiny candle burned in there, and Sam was sitting upright, wide awake, looking at me sad and direct as if he were expecting my call. I was startled.

"Howdy, Sam," I whispered. "Glad you're up. Can I come in?"

Sam motioned with a sweep of a hand for me to enter and sit.

"Nice dancing night, ain't it?" I said. "How come you ain't dancing much these days, Sam?" I planted myself across from him on the dirt floor and inhaled that sweet cedar wood smell that always seemed to surround him.

Sam didn't say anything. He just looked at me with dark, sad eyes.

We set that way for a time, the candle flickering shadows over our faces and the teepee walls. Then Sam spoke.

"Something strong and bad is coming, Nooner Boss," he said.

"Well, something ain't right; I'll say that," I said.

"As the sky changes and as days grow short, Sam sees signs."

"Signs?"

"Bad ahead for many. Sam cannot rest, even if all seems

calm. The wind is wrong. The land is wrong. The journey is wrong. Animals tell Sam of many wrong things past and future."

"Animals?"

"The horse. The lizard. The lacking of the tree birds."

"Hoo-dee-doo, Sam," I said. "I wish you knew English as good as you know critter language."

Sam would not be amused. His mouth got small, and his eyes took on a glare I hadn't seen before. He reached out and gripped my arm. His grasp was strong and painful. His black hair hung down over his face, tonight unbraided.

"Some will die, Nooner Boss," he said. "Perhaps many."

At the moment he clutched my arm, Sam's magic suddenly became very real to me. I could feel his power, and I became aware of an overwhelming pulsation that seemed to pass from him into me as though the blood in his veins was passing into mine. I no longer saw Sam as misshapen and comical. Tonight I looked upon him anew with respect and, for the first time, not a little fear.

An icy wind suddenly howled outside, causing the skins of the teepee to slap loudly. I felt the hairs rise up on the back of my neck. With my free hand I snugged up the collar of Roy's coat tight around my neck.

"Sam will not reach Wickey-Wickey," he said quietly.

"Oh come on, Sam," I said.

He released me then and wrapped his buffalo coat tight around him. He shook his head.

"Nooner Boss knows things are wrong," Sam said. "Nooner Boss feels the coming. Nooner Boss knows. That's why you've come to see Sam." He looked off into a distance at something I couldn't see as though he were in a kind of trance. "Dying we must all do," he said quietly. "But it is in the how of the dying. And it is in the number of the dying. And it is in the reason for the dying. Sam looks for love of Wickey-Wickey. Too late. Nooner Boss has found the golden one. In time. Nooner should leave now. In the night. With the golden one."

"I can't just leave, Sam," I said, alarmed that he would suggest such a thing.

"Nooner Boss must."

"I can't leave," I said stubbornly. "We got us a lost treasure to find, right, Sam? We had us a deal!"

Suddenly, Sam grinned. "Treasure is not lost," he said. "Treasure is always within grasp. But men can never see it for their noses."

"What do you mean?"

Sam shook his head again and touched my shoulder gently. "Nooner has become a friend," he said. "Nooner has become a good friend in many ways."

Then Sam opened his coat and produced his bowie knife from beneath it. He passed the blade slowly from one hand to the other, murmuring quietly. The blade was fat and gleamed in orange and yellow from the light of the small candle. Sam lifted the knife to his throat, pressed it there, and then hooked it under the thong of rawhide from which hung his necklace of gold and bead. With a quick jerk of his hand, he cut the thong and the necklace fell heavily to the earth. Sam picked it up and held it out to me, the beads gleaming and that big gold nugget glowing like a hot coal.

Sam let out a long and tired breath as if the weight of the world had been lifted from his shoulders. I didn't say a word, so transfixed was I. Sam mumbled something more, then stood and tied the necklace around my neck. "Take this," he said. "There is much magic here. Much power."

"Sam, I..."

"Much magic," he said again and squatted down. "Nooner will do great things in his life with this power."

"Sam, I can't take this."

"Yes, Nooner will take. And Nooner must leave Sam and Pine Tree man and preaching man behind."

"I told you, Sam," I said, "I ain't leaving."

Sam stuck his chin at me, angered at my defiance. "Nooner Boss must go! He must!"

I shook my head. "No, Sam."

Sam backed away from me then. His hands were trembling, and he was so angry that I thought he might be tempted to cut my throat ear to ear with his bowie. But then, surprisingly, his face softened and he leaned his head back and started to laugh. He laughed and laughed, long and hard.

"Yes," he said. "Yes, Nooner Boss is strong and wise, but proud and greedy like the mountain lion. I knew Nooner would not go. Nooner is as Sam once was. Foolish. All the young are foolish and bold."

"Sure would be nice if I knew what the hell you're talking about, Sam," I said.

"Nooner Boss knows of what I speak," said Sam. "Nooner Boss feels it. In his heart. Much hardship is coming. Much pain."

"So what else is new," I said, with a bravado that wasn't there.

"If Nooner does not go with the golden one now, then he must do something for Sam."

"Name it," I said.

"He must tell Wickey-Wickey of Sam's great love. He must give the bag of snakes to Wickey-Wickey for Sam. He must tell her I have a great sorrow for what I have done."

"You'll be along," I said. "You can tell her and give her the snakes yourself." I was going to object further, but Sam held up his hand.

"Sam has waited too long," he said, "and is worn down like a rock in a river. Sam has seen pride and anger and foolishness. Sam once could have done great things but was driven to these other things. He has seen his people dwindle and die. Sam is not afraid to die, but Sam, like Nooner Boss, has forgotten things. Now, with death near, Sam remembers."

He hung his head now and looked into the flame of the little candle. The wind howled again outside, blowing beneath the walls of hide that confined us, and I was fearful that the teepee might blow to pieces. Then the wind abated, and I could hear Sam speak again. "If you do not leave with the golden one," he said, "if you do not leave tonight as I ask, then you will do these things for Sam?"

I shuddered. "Yes, I'll do what you ask, but I won't just get up and leave everybody. That I cannot do."

"Yes," Sam said.

Then he blew out the little candle, and we were in pitch blackness. I could hear the grunt and rustle of the old man as he adjusted himself beneath his blanket to sleep. Our meeting was over.

I flapped open the teepee and stepped out into the cold air of the moonlit range. As an afterthought I turned back with the intention of striking up a last-minute argument, but I could see Sam's marble-like eyes still wide and open, reflecting pinpoints of cold moonlight back at me. I shivered, nodded, and walked out.

Strange. When I got outside, I realized that the wind had died, and I found myself wondering if there had ever been a wind at all. In fact the night was so silent now that its stillness seemed to roar.

Chapter 23.

THE COMANCHE NATION

I climbed back into Elishua B.'s wagon, and Hatty was wide awake.

"What's wrong?" she said.

"Nothing. Out to talk to Sam," I told her.

"Something's wrong," she said.

"Nothing's wrong," I lied.

"Sam's acting funny," said Hatty.

"Sam always acts funny," I said.

"You been acting funny too," she said.

"No more funny than usual," I said. I lay down next to her and stroked her forehead with my fingers. "Now close your trap and get some sleep. We've got a long day ahead."

Hatty was quiet for a while, and I thought she was asleep when she spoke again. "We ain't gonna die, are we, Dade?"

I started at the question. "What in hell would make you ask a damn fool thing like that?" I said, with a little more anger in my voice than I had intended.

"Be awfully sad if we did though, wouldn't it?" she said. "After all we've been through?"

"Well, I ain't planning on dying," I said. "But if you keep on, I might just shoot you to get some shut-eye."

Hatty giggled then and snuggled into my arms, and before

long she was snoring. I, on the other hand, spent most of the rest of the night with my eyes wide open and staring, trying to make some sense out of what Sam had told me.

We continued on the next day as the days before. Sam spent a lot of his time climbing trees and standing on high rocks to study the horizon with a red hand fanned over his brow. Neither of us made mention of our conversation the night before.

The knee-high shrub was starting to give way to more and more tree cover, and the flat ground started rounding out in hillocks of apple green and tortilla yellow.

"Comanche camp very close," said Sam. He shook his head and smiled sadly, then headed off on a trot. We kept up with him as best we could.

As usual, Sam was right. A lovely, fertile valley dropped open before us. A quick river flowed through it, and all along and behind this blue ribbon of turbulent water were hundreds of tiny specks that were Comanche dwellings. Beyond the valley jutted a rugged, snow-peaked mountain range. My guess was that this camp held probably a thousand braves or more, the better part of what was left of the Comanche nation.

"My Lord, look at all of them," said Elishua B. "There must be many scores of them."

Pine Top was nervous, but he said nothing.

I looked to Sam. "What now?" I said.

"We wait," he said.

"Wait?"

"We have already been spotted by the Comanche scouts. They will be here soon. We wait."

"But they'll massacre us where we stand," moaned Elishua B., who had a pretty good working knowledge of the Comanche from his travels.

"No, preacher man. Comanche will not kill all of us," said Sam. "They will take you down into the camp to meet the chief. Speak of Wickey-Wickey and the Comanche will know of me."

"I'm scared," said Hatty.

"Not be afraid, golden one," said Sam, although, for once, he wasn't entirely convincing.

And so we waited. And sure enough, true to the words of Sam, we found ourselves surrounded by a party of some dozen painted Comanche braves who appeared out of nowhere with their rifles and arrows trained on us and not looking the least bit glad to see us. They were a healthy but hostile lot, wearing all manner of clothes from top hats to military uniforms to frock coats. I was surprised that they didn't kill us where we stood, but Sam had begun a quiet murmuring which seemed, for the moment, to hold them at bay.

Bravely, Sam addressed the party, indicating the knotted bag of rattlers behind him. The warriors closed in a little more. When they got within ten feet of us, Sam stopped his elocution and crossed his arms. He held his head high, looking over each member of the party as if he were memorizing their faces. Then he made some hand signals, pointed to the bag, and began to speak slowly in a most noble and authoritative voice.

The Comanche looked at Sam in bewilderment, and then at each other. Then one of them said something, pointed at Sam's hump, and some of them started to laugh. Pretty soon, all of them were laughing, and one of them even fell off his pony.

Sam continued to hold his ground standing motionless before them, maintaining his dignity, holding his head high. His fearful expression didn't change, but I could see a glistening tear run slowly down one brown cheek.

I walked up next to him. "What's the matter, Sam?" I said, but he didn't have a chance to answer. Gunfire erupted from somewhere behind us. A Comanche brave fell, and then another, and several more of the Comanche mounts spooked, throwing their riders. Before I could move or even think, Sam hurled himself at me and Hatty, knocking us to the ground. Sam let out a soft moan. His body lurched as bullets hit him, and he clutched, gurgling, at an arrow lodged in his throat. "Take bag," he croaked.

I grabbed the burlap bag of rattlers and dragged Hatty to her feet, and we ran, bullets and arrows zinging all around us. How we managed to keep from getting shot is nothing short of miraculous. Out of the corner of my eye I saw all of our horses scatter, and Pine Top and Elishua B. were nowhere to be seen in the confusion.

Hatty and I were cutting fast through the trees now, and we dove behind a big clump of brush.

Two yipping Comanche fell on us. Hatty screamed, and I managed a Colt loose and fired. One brave fell and the other dove on top of me, knocking my gun away and biting off a chunk of my ear. I wrestled with him and could smell his sweat—his body was slick with it. We were rolling over and over, and this brave was strong and bigger than me and I couldn't get the knife from him, but there was a pop and his forehead blew open in my face, gore gushing, spattering me. The brave went limp and I threw him aside, and there stood Hatty behind him, her little Lightning smoking in her hand.

"What happened? Who started shooting?" Hatty cried.

"I got no idea," I said. "Come on!"

We started running again, Comanche gunfire popping behind us, and we moved as if the devil were after us. We ran as hard as we could into the cover of the trees, me dragging that heavy snake bag behind me. It was absurd. I considered dropping the blasted thing, but I remembered the promise I made to Sam and held to it. Fortunately, the dense brush hindered the progress of the Comanche riders. We found a hollow where I figured we might be safe for a minute or two, and we hurled ourselves into it, puffing and wheezing. I climbed up over the lip of it to take a careful look-see and something hit me hard in the head, sending a dull numbness down my right arm. As I half turned, I was struck again, my head exploding as if lightning was going off in my brain. I groped for purchase but fell, and as I did I caught a horrible glimpse of Hatty lying face down and motionless in the mud of the hollow.

Instinctively I put my hands over my head and tried to explain something, but one more hard, dull thump sent me down into a sickening black and bottomless pool.

Chapter 24.

WICKEY-WICKEY

When I came to, I was tied over the midsection of a bouncing horse like a game animal headed for slaughter. My hands and feet were bound under the belly of the animal, the sweat from its haunches and the taste of my own blood metallic in my mouth. I tried to lift my head to look around but felt sick to my stomach, so I dropped my head but managed to turn it enough to peek behind me. A long line of Comanche warriors and their mounts were following behind. I closed my eyes to play possum, but I just plain passed out instead.

I was jostled conscious as I was dumped to the ground. Something cold splashed in my face. I sputtered and opened my eyes.

I was at the center of the huge Comanche camp, surrounded by dozens of muscular braves. A hundred hostile eyes bore into mine, and as I looked from one face to another, I recognized the pure and silent hatred that the nation was known for. Hatty was lying on her back beside me, blood clotting up around a mean knot on her temple. Her dress was covered with mud and blood and shredded up over her legs, and she was very still.

Then my eyes met those of Roy Roid. He was tied up

across from me, looking at me coldly with a smug smile on his face. He was wearing an Indian loin cloth and little else.

"Hello, Nooner," he said pleasantly.

Pine Top and Elishua B. were tied next to Roy. Elishua B. was sprawled and tied facedown to stakes pounded in the ground, while Pine Top had been lashed to a tree with many loops of hemp coil.

I rolled over and reached for Hatty, and ten Comanche fell on me at once, pinning me flat. I shouted to Hatty as they held me down, and she moaned and moved a little. Then she was still again.

I looked at Pine Top. "She okay?" I shouted over the din of the braves.

Pine Top nodded and shouted back. "I don't think she's hurt bad," he said, "but Sam's dead, Nooner. Sam's dead."

"Oh. Too baaaaad," said Roy Roid from across the way, grinning.

"You son of a bitch," I said. I tried to wrestle free but was held fast by the braves, trussing me tighter yet. "Thanks be to Sam...your brotherhood is now reduced to zero," I said. "And ain't *that* too goddam bad!" I pretended to laugh and couldn't see Roy anymore because of the men around me, but I was pretty sure that I had wiped that sickening smile off Roy's evil face.

A brave cracked me hard with an open hand, said something I couldn't understand, and then spit on the ground. I was delirious with rage. "Awful goddam brave when I'm tied up, you red son of a bitch!" I roared. The warrior hit me again, his hand closed this time. "How come you don't just kill us then, you horse's ass? Or you gonna whack us around for a while? Is that your brilliant Injun plan?"

The braves backed away, watching me with wary

trepidation as though studying a strange and dangerous animal.

"For crying out loud, Nooner! Shut up! Don't get 'em riled!" I recognized Pine Top's warning through the din.

I glared at the braves, and then something like inspiration came over me.

"Wickey-Wickey!" I hollered. "Wickey-Wickey!" I clung to the words like a life rope. "Wickey-Wickey! Wickey-Wickey!" I cried.

Some of the Indians looked mildly surprised. "Wickey-Wickey!" I screeched again. "I want to see Wickey-Wickey!"

The braves began to talk among themselves, gesticulating furiously, murmuring the name. Finally, one of them broke away from the mob and ran off.

The brave came back presently, leading an elderly Indian woman. She was short and slender and lovely to look at in spite of her years. She wore a simple cowhide smock tied at the waist. Her face was a beautiful brown with deep-set dark eyes and long gray hair that she wore in braids tied off at the ends with straw. The brave pointed to her and then to me and said, "Wickey-Wickey." The woman looked at me and trembled. I couldn't blame her. I must have been a helluva sight.

"Wickey-Wickey," I said softly. "Do you speak English?"

She didn't answer.

"English...do you understand? Please...help us," I said.

"No," she said.

"Wickey-Wickey, listen to me. Sam...do you remember Tiptoe Sam? We came with him. He came to find you." I thought for a moment that I saw a glimmer of melancholy recognition in her expression. "He was killed up on the ridge just now."

I reached to my neck and pulled aside the scarf that

I wore to hide the necklace Sam had given me. Wickey-Wickey's eyes widened in amazement when she saw it, and she pressed a fist into her mouth. She leaned down to me and touched the golden nugget with her long fingers.

"Sam gave this to me," I said. "Do you remember it?"

Wickey-Wickey turned and ran away, sobbing.

Chapter 25.

MUKAPON

The Comanche chief was a tall, arrogant, and physically striking youth with a powerful presence. He was young for a chief; I was to learn that his leadership was recent as his father had died just months before. As a result he was full of the fire, impatience, and uncertainty of any young man unexpectedly burdened with authority and responsibility.

He had been on a hunt with a handful of braves when we had gotten into the skirmish with his warriors. Now back among his people, the young chief stood before them looking as noble and wise as he could, his strong arms crossed resolutely over his chest. He looked down upon us with disgust and anger. Several of his braves were dead, and we had invaded his territory without being provoked. Now, it seemed, he was going to make us suffer for it.

"You will die with much pain for the killing of my people," he said in clear, careful English.

"It wasn't us that shot your boys, Chief," I babbled. "It was him!" I pointed at Roy. "That thieving, bloodthirsty bastard over there! He's the one did the killing of your braves."

"He would cloud your mind with lies, Mighty Chief," said Roy easily, his voice smooth as silk. "This man killed my brothers, and he killed your brave men when they got in his way."

"Not true, Chief!" I shouted. "We came to the Comanche in peace to find Wickey-Wickey. Tiptoe Sam brought us here. The man who speaks yonder is a cowardly killer of men from all nations."

The chief's nostrils flared and his eyes grew guarded. "How do you know of Wickey-Wickey?" he demanded.

"Wickey-Wickey was Sam the Apache's lover long ago," I said.

It was the wrong thing to say. The young chief became livid with outrage. He drew a knife from a sheath that hung on his waist, yanked my head up by a handful of hair, and pressed the knife to my throat. "You lie!" he shouted. "Like all the white men, you lie! Wickey-Wickey is my mother!"

"Lord Almighty," said Elishua B.

But suddenly a voice pierced the camp, a woman's voice, clear and commanding.

"He does not lie," said the voice. "Leave him!"

Warriors, maidens, and braves alike stood aside as the elderly Wickey-Wickey strode among us.

"Look at the stone the white rider wears," she told the young chief. "You will see the truth."

Reluctantly, the young chief sheathed his knife, then tore my bandana aside and saw the gold nugget necklace hanging beneath. He looked upon it scornfully. Comanche words were exchanged—the chief angry, other braves arguing, Wickey-Wickey speaking in an imploring tone. The chief looked at Wickey-Wickey, then at the necklace. He dropped to his knees and cupped the nugget in his hands, and a general babble of wonder rose among the population.

Suddenly the chief tore the necklace from my neck. "Where did you get this?" he snarled.

"It is from your great treasure, Chief, the stones of color. It is a rock of gold given me by Tiptoe Sam the Apache, the man your braves have killed upon the ridge."

"His name was not Tiptoe Sam, white rider," said

Wickey-Wickey. "Tiptoe Sam was the name given him by the white man to scorn him. His name was Mukapon."

A great hush suddenly fell over the Indians. Some could be heard repeating the name in whispers: Mukapon.

The young chief started at the utterance of the name. "Mukapon?" he said, and his voice had both wonder and fear in its inflection. "Mukapon of the ghost dancers?"

"Yes," said Wickey-Wickey, "the same. The great Mukapon, exiled by his own tribe because he held strange powers that none could understand. Mukapon, ridiculed and feared because he was misshapen. Mukapon, whose love for a Comanche maiden, *this* Comanche maiden, was condemned and forbidden. In his loneliness and anger, Mukapon stole the stones of color from the Comanche many years ago. And I was Mukapon's woman before your father, Riding Wing."

"You, Mother?" said the chief in disbelief. "But Mukapon was a bandit, an outlaw! A devil who would steal the wealth of a nation! I wish I had killed him myself!"

"No!" shouted Wickey-Wickey. "Mukapon was a great lone warrior. He did much for the Apache and the Comanche nations, and yet still they turned their backs on him. Give the white rider back the stone as Mukapon intended!"

The young chief scowled. "If it is of the treasure of our ancestors, it belongs to the Comanche. If once it belonged to Mukapon, then it has much power. Such power is worthy only of a chief."

"Give the white rider back the stone," said Wickey-Wickey again. "If Mukapon saw fit to give it to the white rider, then the white rider should possess it."

The chief studied the golden nugget. Then, angrily, he hurled it back at me.

"Have your stone, devil," he said.

"He ain't no devil, goddammit," said Pine Top in angry frustation. "That Roy Roid over there, he's your devil!"

"Close your mouth, large one!" snarled the Comanche

chief to Pine Top.

Roy sat, silent and grinning, pleased with the hostility and confusion he had created.

"Wickey-Wickey," I said, "please listen to me. Sam... Mukapon wanted me to give you a message for him. And a gift. It is a strange gift, but it was very important to him that you have it. It's a big bag of rattlesnakes, resting yonder, up on the ridge where he was killed."

"A bag of rattlesnakes, pah!" said the chief, scornfully. "What good is a bag of snakes?"

"Mukapon would give me snakes?" said Wickey-Wickey in bewilderment.

"I don't know why," I said, "but it was important to Mukapon that you have them. I gave him my word."

Suddenly a strange, warm feeling overwhelmed me as I sat, and as I held the nugget in my hands, it began to glow and warm to the touch.

"He is a devil, wise chief," said Roy again, his voice still cool and reassuring. "He is the one who steals your treasure. You see? He wears your stone! What more proof do you need? He who offers snakes as a gift to a woman. Ha! Who else but a devil would carry snakes and ride with a ghost-dancing devil Apache?"

The young chief regarded Roy in somber consideration.

"And this man is even marked as a devil," continued Roy in his greasy tone. "He speaks with the devil's tongue. Don't let his evil powers fool you. Look at his face, Chief. He is marked. His face is slashed. He is marked as a devil."

"The only devil here is you, you murderous nutbag," I shouted. "Chief! Listen to me! This man here is known for murdering men everywhere, all across the plain. For fun! And he wears a lady's panty! You got to ask yourself one question, Chief: what kind of a crazy son of a bitch likes to murder people and wear a lady's lacy panty?"

"Silence!" shouted the young chief, now in absolute and

complete confusion. He strode over to me, squatted down, and looked at me incredulously as though I were insane. He studied my face. He ran a thick thumb over the scars in my cheeks. Then he stood upright, crossed his arms, and considered the strange balance of the equation.

"There is only one way to settle this," the chief finally said, "only one way to find the truth."

"No!" cried Wickey-Wickey.

"It is the only way," the chief said again. He barked orders, and Wickey-Wickey struggled in protest as several braves led her away.

Roy's horrible grin widened. Lordy, we were in it now. Things were looking pretty grim overall for all of us here at this particular juncture, I got to say.

Chapter 26.

FIGHT TO THE DEATH

Night fell, but there was little relief in it. I was sweating like a bull, and stinging mosquitoes and gnats buzzed around my head, attracted to my blood. My head throbbed, and it hurt me in the chest to breathe. Everywhere my body was sore, cut, bloody, and swelled up. I was, in short, one miserable son of a bitch.

Under careful guard, the chief ordered all of us untied one at a time and allowed us to eat.

"They're fattening us to eat us," moaned Elishua B. Tombatu.

"Aw c'mon, Elishua B.," said Pine Top. "Injuns don't eat people. Even I know that."

Roy smirked at us from across the way. "Such a clever bunch," he said.

"You're the one decided to take potshots at the whole god-dam Comanche nation," I said.

"Anything to accomplish your demise," said Roy, working his fingers and cracking the knuckles of his big hands.

"You ain't done it yet, shitcake," I said.

"We'll see," Roy said, smiling that horrific, empty smile of his. "Oh yes. We'll see."

I sidled over toward Hatty. "How you holdin', girl?" I asked her. She had come to consciousness a couple hours previous, and save for the cuts and bruises that I could see, she was doin' admirably well, considering.

"What's gonna happen, Dade?" she said, trying to stay calm.

"I don't know, Hatty," I said. "Hell, I just don't know what we're in for."

After we had all supped and drunk, the young chief approached us. He now wore a simple loincloth. "You are fed, you are rested," he said simply. "Now you will fight."

"Fight?" I said wearily. "You kiddin' me, Chief? Again?"

"You and this man," said the young chief, pointing at Roy, "will battle to determine who speaks the truth."

"Oh, is that all," I sighed. "Boy howdy, Chief, you sure make it tough on a guy."

Roy, of course, was pleased at the notion. "Yesss," I could hear him say. "Yesss."

"A battle to the death," said the chief.

I looked across at Roy. "I will fight this man, Chief," I said. "But first you bring Mukapon's body down from that ridge and get that bag of snakes here to Wickey-Wickey."

The chief considered this proposal for a moment, eyeing my necklace covetously.

"What you ask is craziness," the chief spat. "But after the fight, if you win, we will honor your craziness. But, if you do not win, we will take the golden woman. We will take the black preaching man and the giant bearded one, and they will die slowly in fire. Mukapon's body will be beheaded and burned."

"Oh God, Dade," said Hatty.

The Comanche throng lifted all of us upright and walked us limping into a clearing at the center of the camp beside a roaring bonfire. There was much spitting and abuse by the braves along the way. Elishua B.'s wagon was there in the clearing looking like a pincushion on account of it having so many arrows stuck in it. A young brave had been assigned the job of retrieving the arrows from it. One at a time he wiggled them loose and stuck them into his quiver. He looked angrily at me, peeved at having been designated the task and blaming me for the trouble.

Silently the Comanche braves surrounded Roy and me, and the two of us squared off in the middle of the clearing. Between us, the chief laid a double-edged dagger and walked us opposite one another about ten paces. Then, without further ceremony, he and another brave cut our hands loose, and the braves began to whoop.

I was slow, but Roy wasn't. He dove on the knife quick as a cat, then rolled upright with it and grinned. He ran at me, we collided, and I caught the blade in my hand as the point lurched toward my midsection. My palm got hot and slick with blood as I tried to hold it off, and Roy lurched with it again and again, sawing my palms to ribbons as he thrust it toward my belly. I had both hands on the knife, but I knew I couldn't sheath it much longer. Roy was smiling, and his breath was hot and smelled like garbage. I could see his eyes and that cold stare of his, and I leaned into him, opened my mouth wide, and bit off a piece of his face. He screamed, dropped the knife, and fell back, clutching a bloody stump with both hands where most of his nose used to be.

I spat out a bloody wad the size of my thumb and fell on him, and we rolled, punching and flailing and gouging each other in the dirt and blood. He managed to get his big hands around my neck and started squeezing, squeezing, ramming his big thumbs hard into my Adam's apple. I was seeing spots and fighting for air, but somehow I managed to get him by the hair and pulled him across the clearing, bashing his head hard against an iron bracket mounted on the side of Elishua B.'s wagon. Roy's head split open and his grip relaxed, but as he fell he brought a knee up hard into my pod. I yelped like a dog and rolled double away, and he tumbled off and staggered toward the fire.

He fought to his feet as I pulled myself weakly up the side of the wagon, exhausted and dizzy, blood covering my hands and arms. Roy gurgled something at me from across the fire through a red mask of raw angry gore, but I couldn't hear what he said. In the firelight I could see the wide eyes of the Comanche braves that surrounded us watching, shouting, waiting.

Roy spotted the knife on the ground and pounced on it. I was too weak and too tired to stop him. Then he picked up a flaming limb from the fire and slowly, deliberately, came at me again. He looked like a demon, his face an ugly explosion of spurting black blood. "You die, Nooner," he said, grinning crazily, blood and spit running down his face in thick rivulets. "You die."

Delirious, I groped inside the wagon, looking for some-thing—anything—that I could use to defend myself. I came up with a handful of Hatty's clothes, an old boot, a Bible, and a bottle of Elishua B.'s Miracle Tonic. Roy was within a few feet of me now, moving in for the kill, poking at me with the knife and swinging at me with the burning limb. I ducked, and the flaming kindling clipped my head. I threw the Bible hard at Roy and it caught him square in his nose stump. He let out a shriek and staggered back a few steps. Then I broke the bottle of Miracle Tonic open on the side of the wagon and in one mo-tion threw the contents of the bottle in his face.

Roy let out an ungodly scream as his face and head erupt-ed in a glorious ball of searing blue fire.

Chapter 27.

RATTLER BAG

Nobody bothered to put Roy out, least of all me. I watched emptily as he ran shrieking around the camp, his hysterical movements only serving to fan the flames that now thoroughly consumed his head. He clutched and slapped at his face with his hands, his hair and flesh sizzling and snapping and blackening. The smell was something terrible. Finally Roy stopped his running. His body shivered and wiggled, and as his legs gave out, he collapsed into a comical squat. Still he twitched and spasmed, his head a golden ball of orange. Soon he was entirely still, just sitting there hunched on the ground until not much more than a black, smoking, grinning skull remained on his shoulders.

The Comanche were silent now. They watched as I staggered, screaming and bleeding, to Elishua B's wagon. I dug around and found an ax handle. Then I approached what was left of Roy Roid's squatting corpse and swung the ax handle as hard as I could, again and again and again, hammering what was left of Roy's head into a pulp of charred skull and brain. With each devastating blow, the Comanche shouted, the women cried out. When his head was completely pulverized, I threw the dripping ax handle into the fire, staggered back to the wagon, and found another bottle of tonic. I uncorked the

LAINE SCHELIGA PRESENTS...

bottle and took a long draw from it. Then I slid down the side of the wagon to my butt and passed out.

By this time the chief, true to his word, had ordered Hatty and Pine Top and Elishua B. set free. They all rushed to my side.

"Nooner!" said Pine Top, pouring water over my head and then giving me a drink from a water bag. "Oh God, Nooner!"

"He's dead," I said feverishly. "Roy...he's finally dead."

Elishua B. picked up the Bible, which sat on the ground, and he looked up to the heavens. "Oh Lord," he said.

"Dade, your hands..." Hatty said.

"Huh?" I said. I looked down at shocking flesh that hung in strips from my trembling hands. "Guess I won't be dealing Faro anytime soon," I said.

The young chief approached, unsettled.

"White rider speaks the truth," he said, his voice, I thought, quavering.

"Brilliant work, Chief," I said weakly. "Yee-haw."

"You bit his nose off," said Pine Top in wonder. "I ain't never seen nobody bite nobody's nose off before."

Pine Top lifted me into his arms and carried me gently over to the bank of the river where, upon the orders of the chief, I was stripped buck naked and washed like a little baby by a handful of Indian maidens. Hatty didn't like it much, but she had nothing to say about it, and I was too far gone to enjoy it anyhow. My bloody clothes were removed and burned in the bonfire, and seeing as they were Roy's clothes, it seemed only right they were destroyed. My wounds were rinsed and treated with poultices and weeds, and wrapped up by a Comanche medicine man who was a funny old guy, all elbows and kneecaps but with delicate and clever hands. The young chief brought me a ceremonial loincloth doodad to wear into which they tucked my two amigos and my dangler when I was dried off. Wickey-Wickey brought out a pair of chamois moccasins for me and carefully put them on my feet.

◆ 130 ◆

Then Pine Top carried me to a place in the camp where I would be left alone. Hatty rocked me gently to sleep by a fire.

Late the next day I awakened about as wracked and broken and stiff and twisted and torn as I have ever been in all my born days. I wanted to die. My head and hand wrappings were sopped and hard with congealed blood. The events of the previous night came to me like a horrible dream, and I could do nothing to quell the horror of what I had done. My throat was bruised black and blue all the way 'round from Roy Roid's big hands.

I was saddened, too, on account of I had lost my friend Sam. And I had lost Shithead and my saddle and my favorite boots and my Peacemakers that my daddy, Dude Nooner, give me and all my clothes and everything else of a material nature that I had in the world besides. Perhaps, too, I had lost my mind. But I kept this consideration close to me and suffered many, many sleepless nights to come.

At least I had my life left, I figured, such as it was. And I had rid the world of that turd Roy Roid, and maybe now Hatty would be safe for a while and Pine Top would be okay, too, and maybe Elishua B. might have a chance to make some coin selling some of his remaining Miracle Tonic inventory to the Comanche.

But I knew that there was one thing left to be done, and that was to fulfill my last promise to Sam. After that I was due for a good long rest somewhere with Hatty if she would have me. I wondered how anyone would want me after how disfigured I was, not to mention the horrors I had committed on Roy Roid that terrible night.

Everybody was already up and around when I crawled up, anguish stricken, onto my elbows. My hands hurt me terribly, the pain unlike anything I have ever known. I could only steel myself to it and suffer quietly. The medicine man provided me with tonics and herbs that seemed to quell the pain a little. Otherwise, I could do nothing but lie still for many days, and that I did.

Finally, when I could move without screaming, when I could look people in the eye and move without shame, I sent for the chief.

He came to me with Wickey-Wickey.

"How do you do today, white rider?" he said carefully.

"They call me Nooner," I said, "and I feel like I've been dragged naked across the United States over broken glass and then dipped in whiskey, if you want to know the truth, Chief," I said.

"I am sorry to have caused this," said the young chief with some shame in his voice. "I am very sorry for the paining of the Nooner."

"Don't mind it, Chief," I said. "Don't mind it."

"Something I can do to help? Something you wish?"

"Send a couple of braves up to that ridge and ask them to go back to the hollow where they bushwhacked me and bring that bag of rattlers back to camp."

The chief looked uncertain, but nodded and gave the order.

"Them snakes don't make no difference now, do they, Nooner?" said Pine Top.

"I don't know," I said helplessly. "They made a lot of difference to Sam for some reason. I made him a promise. I intend to keep it."

It wasn't long before four braves returned, dragging ol' Tiptoe Sam's big, knotted burlap snake bag between them.

"Where is Mukapon's body?" I asked.

The chief spoke with his braves a moment. "They say there is no body to be found," he said.

"That can't be," I said. "I saw him with my own eyes. He was plenty dead. Layin' up there on the ridge."

"He is not there now."

I looked at Wickey-Wickey, and she smiled. I caught something in her expression. "Where is he?" I asked her quietly.

Tears pooled in her eyes. "Do not worry. He is taken care of."

"Mukapon loved you very much, Wickey-Wickey," I told her. "He wanted me to tell you that. He knew that something bad was going to happen and that he had done the wrong thing by you and your people."

"I know," she said. "He was a very powerful man, a fine and brave man. But a very sad man in many ways, too."

"I think he felt better knowing that I would see you. He wanted me to tell you that he knew he had made many mistakes, and he wanted you to have this bag of rattlesnakes."

Four braves lumbered over carrying Sam's burlap sack. They could barely handle it for it seemed cumbersome and heavy. They dropped it on the ground before us, and something rattled inside.

Wickey-Wickey looked at the big sack, and as she did, I got the most curious lightheaded sensation, and I thought I caught a whiff of fresh cedar somewhere on the air.

"What am I to do with this, a bag of snakes?" Wickey-Wickey wondered aloud.

"I don't know," I said. "I thought you would know."

"I do not," she said.

"Maybe you could cook them rattlers up or make a hat out of them or something," Pine Top offered.

Wickey-Wickey leaned over and tried to pick up the bag, but it was much too heavy. As she disturbed the bag, it fell open. Frightened, she jumped away from it, expecting rattlers to come slithering out of the opening, but instead, something blue and shiny tumbled out. I leaned over and picked it up. It was a fine piece of rich blue turquoise infused with silver, about the size of an apple.

"Lordy," I said, turning the beautiful stone over and over in my hands.

I kicked at the bag a couple of times. Whatever was inside wasn't snakes. I carefully grabbed the bottom of the hemp sack and gave it a tentative shake. With a swish, a thousand natural crystalline rocks of agate and sapphire and ruby and amber tumbled glittering out of that bag. Uncut diamonds set in silica came out of that bag. Pieces of gold set in quartz and indescribably beautiful polished worry stones of marble and naturally fused ingots of great beauty tumbled forth out of that bag. Ancient fossils of creatures preserved in hardened mud and bits of petrified wood and bone and unbelievable geodes and other carefully polished geological treasures of all kinds in all forms and in all colors tumbled away and out of that bag.

"The stones of color," I gasped.

Chapter 28.

ADIOS

Hatty, Pine Top, Elishua B., and me from that day forth were regarded as folk heroes by the Comanche, who had, because of us, become rejoined with the natural wealth of their ancestors. Wickey-Wickey and the young chief made gifts to us all from the magnificent abundance discovered in Sam's rattler bag.

Pine Top got some small nuggets of gold and some pretty mineral rocks that he liked real well, and Elishua B. was given some tumbled metamorphic stones and a whole pile of crystalline minerals, all of which he would later sell as mystic tokens at a fantastic profit.

Hatty and I were presented with a fat pouch of gold dust and several of the largest gold nuggets from the stones of color.

We stayed in the Comanche encampment another week or so, until one day, when my head had settled somewhat and my hands had healed enough for me to almost hold fast the reins of a horse, I decided it was time that Hatty and me said adios. Truly, we could stay no longer. We had our lives to live and figured we had places to go. We didn't quite know where those places were just yet, but that didn't seem to matter at the time. We just knew we had to move along.

We loaded a couple of horses with provisions and gear,

and got ready one fine morning. Big ol' Pine Top got to sniveling and crying when I told him of our intention to leave, and he put his big old hairy arms around me and pushed his big old, stinky, raggedy-ass beard into my face and squeezed me so hard to his barrel chest that I thought my head might pop right off.

"How come you got to go, Nooner?" he said. "Things are good here."

"Things are good," I said, "but Hatty and I, we need to move along. We got things we got to do, just the two of us, I reckon. Besides," I said, "you got something of your own to start with now, Pine Top. And you're still bulletproof besides."

"Well, I don't know," Pine Top said. "Bulletproof or not, you done saved my life and all."

"Me and Hatty got some ridin' to do. Maybe we'll be settling down someplace and building up a little homestead for ourselves." I looked down at my hands. "Besides, I don't expect to be doing much shooting or riding or roping or much of anything in the near future anyways."

"You ain't no homesteader," snorted Pine Top. "You're a rough and ready lone wolf."

"Well, maybe I could give it a try anyhow," I said. "Ain't much else I ain't tried."

"Aw hell, I'm gonna miss you, ol' Nooner," he said.

"Me too, amigo," I said. "But we'll meet again; I know we will."

And Pine Top sobbed a big old baby sob and hugged me again.

Elishua B. was much more understanding of our need to depart, in spite of the hospitality of the Comanche. He was, in fact, preparing to take leave, too. "I'll be thinking of you, Nooner," said Elishua B., "each night as I roam these unforgiving plains. I'll play 'Sweet Beckoning Sue' from time to time in order that I might fully refresh the memory of your fine acquaintance."

Days later, I was to discover that Elishua B. had stowed his blood-smeared Bible and several bottles of his Miracle Tonic into my saddlebag. I made a mental note to do a little reading of Elishua B.'s Good Book now and again, instead of reading just those nickel cowboy books all the time. Just for a change of perspective, you understand.

The chief and Wickey-Wickey came to see us off too. "You have the thanks of all our people," the young chief said. "You will be honored, and the story of your bravery will be told. To stay with the Comanche in our territory," said the chief, "you have but to come. The Comanche people will know you by the necklace you wear. If you are ever in trouble or need, you have but to ask and we will come."

All in all, in my estimation, it was the finest promise ever made to a white man by a hostile Comanche leader, and I knew that the young chief would be good to his word.

I lifted my hat in a final farewell, and with that, Hatty and I rode off together and out of the Comanche encampment the way we had come.

Chapter 29.

RECKONING

Hatty was swatting with girlish impatience at a fly that was buzzing around her head. "Well, here we are back on the damn trail," she said irritably.

"Yep," I said, grinning. "Ain't it grand?"

She looked at me and then smiled in spite of herself. "Yes. I suppose it is, ain't it, Dade?"

And we rode, not knowing exactly where we were headed, and yet, somehow, knowing. I had some things I knew I still had to tend to, but for once I wasn't in a hurry, and I had a clarity of resolution that was tempered by a feeling of great contentment and a sense of wonderful and unexplainable connectedness, if you will. I can't rightly explain this disposition, but it produced in me a bright outlook in spite of my many debilitating injuries.

And it was especially good that Hatty was there with me. It was difficult for me to ride for very long, and she cared for me with great patience and a never-flagging tenderness.

As we traveled, we spoke of our adventures as they had unfolded and tried to make some sense out of it all. The business of how the bag of snakes turned out to be the stones of color...well, it was a magic we figured—a magic that only Sam would ever completely understand. An elusive puzzle it is indeed, and one which we haven't been able to figure on completely, even to this day.

Hatty and I loved on each other much, and eventually I gave her the ring that I wore on my little finger—the silver one with the black stone scarab bug from Egyptia that Elishua B. Tombatu had given me many months before. This token suggestion of marriage seemed to quell Hatty's anxieties on the subject. If I had known before that a little bitty ring would have such a profoundly reassuring effect on her, why, I would have given her one a long time ago just to get her to quiet down some.

We rode. And pretty soon, we found ourselves riding upon that poor Cherokee camp where Chief Whatever the Hell His Name Is was. As we rode in, Little Bear Foot came running up to us and I waved, and he sort of waved back. I gave him a piece of quartz from my pocket, and he actually smiled; then Deer Leaping Over the Pond came up and asked me what we thought we wanted.

"I want to see Chief Whatever the Hell His Name Is again, Deer," I said. I tossed him a bottle of Elishua B.'s tonic. "I couldn't get you no whiskey, Deer, but this here's something a little better."

Deer's cheeks got even more apple red than they already were. "Thank you, white rider," he said.

"They call me Nooner," I said. "And don't mention it, Deer."

Hatty looked at me funny. "What's the matter with you, Dade?" she wanted to know. "How come you're calling this Indian 'dear'?"

"Oh, Jesus howdy, Hatty," I said, exasperated. "It's his name."

Deer Leaping Over the Pond showed us to the teepee of the chief.

"Chief is in tent sleeping a comfy nap," Deer Leaping Over the Pond said.

"Wake him, will you?" I said. "I have news."

Deer did. He ushered us into the teepee and scampered off with his treasure.

"You have returned," said the old chief, yawning and stretching and eyeballing Hatty with some misgiving. "Hello, Golden One," he said gruffly. "Boring in teepee all day."

"I have some very bad news," I told him.

"News is always very bad these days," he said.

"Sam is dead, Chief. He was killed some weeks ago. I know you were his goodly friend, and, well, I figured you'd want to know."

The old chief hung his head and his eyes filled with tears. "Sam knew it was to come," he finally said. "He told me himself. But Sam will live beyond his years."

"Yes he will," I said.

"Many thanks for the coming," he said.

"It was the least we could do, Chief," I said. "Hatty wanted to return that paint she took, too."

I pulled a gold nugget from my pouch. "And I want you to take this nugget and get yourselves some horses and take care of things some. I'm sure Sam would have wanted that."

The chief smiled around his tears. "Many thanks are yours," he said.

"And me and Hatty here would like you to teach us a rain dance before we go."

"You would?" he said happily.

"I figure if we're going to settle down to bustin' sod, we're gonna need to be able to get us some rainfall from time to time."

Naturally the old chief was most delighted, and we spent the rest of that day taking rain dance lessons and enjoying the company and hospitality of the Cherokee. I spent a good deal of the time showing the younger Indians how to play gambling card games and how to deal a deck in favor of themselves. They found particular interest in my explanations of card trickery and the arithmetics of probability. Most of all, I think they were best pleased with the potential for separating men from their money using odds and opportunity to their advantage. They seemed to catch on quick.

It didn't rain the next morning, even after all our rain dancing, much to the dismay of the chief, so Hatty and I said our goodbyes and decided to light out east. After a few days of hard and protracted riding, we came upon a cloud of dust that sure enough was being made by that crazy, old, prospecting dirt-digger prick, Dandy Dan, that I had met before in my travels.

As we approached him, I noticed that the old bastard was wearing my poncho and my boots and my shirt and my hat and my britches, and he was wrestling with Shithead on account of Shithead didn't like him any better than I did and was in fact taking bites out of the old coot's flat butt as the horse tried to bust halter.

"Well howdy, you thieving ball sack," I said to him, laughing at him until my sides hurt. "Find any fricking gold yet?"

Dandy Dan didn't look up because Shithead was keeping him busy, all excited at seeing me and chomping at the bit and all, fighting and biting at the old-timer to get away.

Finally, Shithead broke loose and ran toward us. When that old-timer looked up, he saw who I was and almost loaded my britches right there and then.

I pulled a weapon from my saddle and pointed it at him. "Now before you get any ideas of your own, you old bag of dirt, supposing you just take off them clothes and boots and drop them britches right there where you stand. That's right, old-timer, just drop 'em right off."

"Goddam young puncher," he snarled. "I'll be nekked."

"There's that," I said, fanning back the hammer.

Without more argument, Dandy Dan took off all my duds and dropped them there in the creek bed. His old body was all white and wrinkly, and I noticed that Hatty was getting an eyeful of Dandy Dan's little dingus hanging out tender in the sun.

Hatty got off her horse, walked over, and picked up all my clothes and weapons and such; then comes back over and puts the gear in a saddlebag. Shithead sidled up next to me, and I pat his big old dumbass head, being careful not to let my fingers get too close to his teeth. I grabbed his reins and pulled him alongside my mount, and I saw that my good old holster and my daddy's Peacemakers were there, hanging on the pommel of my good old saddle.

"You ain't gonna leave a poor ol' man out here all nekked an' all, are ya?" cried Dandy Dan as we fixed to leave.

"There's that," I said again.

"Well, what the hell am I gonna do now? That there damn horse o' yours done chewed up all my old clothes!"

"Patience," I told the old-timer. I tossed something at him. "Put that on if you need something to wear."

The old-timer held up Hatty's ripped-up blue dress.

"This here's a dress!" cried Dandy Dan. "I can't be wearing no dang dress."

"Sure you can," I told him. "Who knows? You might like it. I know I did."

Hatty giggled and mounted up.

"See you around, Dandy Dan," I said. "I wish you luck, 'cause you're gonna need a lot of it. And you better keep your thieving self real clear of me from here on out. If I see one hair on your stinkin' head, your ass and that gold pan of yours are gonna have some extra holes in 'em."

And off we rode.

Years later, I was to hear of Dandy Dan again. It seems that eventually he got the hang of prospecting and actually struck gold. With the proceeds, he ended up purchasing a saloon in Texas that featured dancing fancy men dressed up to look like ladies. Apparently the novelty of the idea was quite popular for a while, and the enterprise did very well until it was burned to the ground by a confused and angry group of cowpunchers fresh in from Nebraska.

Chapter 30.

TREASURE

Hatty and I got to riding again with Shithead in tow, and we soon found ourselves in that pretty little place where I saw her that time when we were swimming naked in the creek with the beavers and the trout fishes beneath the cool cedar trees.

We dismounted to drink from the creek. "I like this place," I said, splashing the water over my head and feeling overall invigorated and pleased. "I think that this might be a good place to get things started."

"Things is already started," said Hatty softly.

I tied the horses to some trees and then lifted her off her horse and into my arms. "My Lord but you're getting heavy," I said.

"Ain't I though," she said slyly.

"Must be all that good food you been making," I said.

"Could be," she said, grinning. "But I don't think so."

I looked at her face all especially pretty and soft and smiling in the shade of that splendid place, and I felt a strange and wonderful realization tingle through me.

"Well now," I said as I set her down gently to earth. "Well now, well now, well now." And that was about all I could think of to say at the time.

We lay together in that pretty shaded place and held each other for a long time. Hatty slept quietly, and as the day fell to twilight, I took a little walk to study the landscape. I figured we might be staying here for a while. A little breeze kicked up as I walked, and suddenly I caught the scent of fresh-cut cedar on the air. I noticed the water and watched how it gurgled clear and clean and cold over the rocks, and my heart felt glad. I heard the leaves rustle gentle above, and for a moment I thought I saw someone standing in the shadowed distance among the trees, arms crossed, watching.

"Sam?" I shouted. I ran over to the spot, but of course no one was there.

Then at that moment, as darkness fell to completion, I heard a sound carried by the wind. It could have been the movement of the branches in the wind through the high trees, but it wasn't that. It was a distant howling, the baying of an animal. I cocked my head for a better listen, and I knew immediately what was making the sound.

It was a wolf I figured, howling in the night. And somehow I knew that that wolf was not crying in sadness or fear or desperation or predation. I knew that wolf was howling in a kind of joy tonight because he was back in the company of a lost companion. I knew that wolf was howling because he was joyous in the new night, joyous ultimately and finally. Joyous because he was home.

"Well, I'll be," I said aloud. I walked back to Hatty and lay next to her and pulled her close to me beside the fire, which burned a soft orange-yellow now, there in the cover of them whispering, sweet-smelling cedars.

"Umma-umma-umma," I said to myself contentedly. Then, without another thought or word, I fell deeply and happily asleep.

THE END

Lightning Source UK Ltd.
Milton Keynes UK
UKHW041139150622
404467UK00001B/40